A Visit to Priapus and Other Stories

A Visit to Priapus

AND

OTHER STORIES

Glenway Wescott

Edited
and with an introduction
by

Jerry Rosco

The University of Wisconsin Press

The University of Wisconsin Press
1930 Monroe Street, 3rd Floor
Madison, Wisconsin 53711-2059
uwpress.wisc.edu

3 Henrietta Street
London WC2E 8LU, England
eurospanbookstore.com

Published by arrangement with the Estate of Glenway Wescott,
Anatole Pohorilenko, literary executor, c/o Harold Ober Associates Incorporated

Printed in the United States of America

Library of Congress Cataloging-in-Publication Data

Wescott, Glenway, 1901–1987, author.
[Short stories. Selections]
A visit to Priapus and other stories / Glenway Wescott; edited and
with an introduction by Jerry Rosco.
p.   cm.
ISBN 978-0-299-29690-2 (cloth: alk. paper)
ISBN 978-0-299-29693-3 (e-book)
I. Rosco, Jerry, editor.   II. Title.
PS3545.E827V57   2013
813′.52—dc23
2013010427

"The Stallions," "An Example of Suicide," and "Sacre de Printemps" are previously unpublished.
"Adolescence" was first published in *Goodbye, Wisconsin*, copyright © 1928, 1955 by Glenway
Wescott. "A Visit to Priapus" was first published in *The New Penguin Book of Gay Short Stories*,
copyright © 2003 by Anatole Pohorilenko. "The Odor of Rosemary" was first published in *Prose*
(Spring 1971), copyright © 1971 by Glenway Wescott. "The Valley Submerged" was first published
in *The Southern Review* (Summer 1965), copyright © 1965 by Glenway Wescott. "The Babe's Bed"
was first published by Harrison of Paris (1930). "Mr. Auerbach in Paris" (April 1942) and "The
Frenchman Six Feet Three" (July 1942) were first published in *Harper's*. "The Love of New York"
was first published in *Harper's Bazaar* (December 1943). "A Call on Colette and Goudeket" was
first published in *Town and Country* (January 1953).

Contents

Foreword

WENDY MOFFAT

The British novelist E. M. Forster would be posthumously delighted that these stories by Glenway Wescott have found a public audience. "A Visit to Priapus" now joins Forster's *The Life to Come and Other Stories* and *Maurice*, worthy writing on gay themes that was suppressed for decades as "the penalty society exacts" for its hatred and fear of homosexuals. The publication of these stories by Wescott marks a "happier year."[1]

Wescott revered Forster the man, his art, and his powerful humanistic vision. His novels, including *A Room with a View*, *Howards End*, and *A Passage to India* had established him internationally as a great man of letters. Wescott and Forster met in the 1940s at an auspicious time for both men. Forster, almost seventy, finally felt free to live a more open life after his mother's death. Wescott, a generation younger, was a relentlessly exacting writer whose early celebrity had somewhat faded. But the renewed critical success of *The Pilgrim Hawk* (1940) encouraged Wescott. He had begun to write the searingly honest stories in this collection.

---

1. E. M. Forster, "Notes on *Maurice*," in *Maurice*, ed. Philip Gardner (London: Andre Deutsch, 1999), 216. "To a happier year" is Forster's dedicatory phrase for the novel. Forster's "Notes" were written in 1960.

To Wescott, Forster was a cross between a *paterfamilias* and a patron saint of gay writing. The myth that the old man had written a gay love story with a happy ending, written it decades before, even before World War I, circulated seductively among Wescott's New York friends. In 1949 Wescott parlayed a decade of correspondence into an invitation for Forster to visit the United States. To Wescott's delight Forster brought along his partner, the policeman Bob Buckingham. The couple spent a weekend at Wescott's country house and enjoyed a notably ribald and frank dinner party in the company of Wescott, his partner Monroe Wheeler, and the sexologist Dr. Alfred Kinsey.

During Forster's visit, Wescott learned the whole story of the writing and suppression of *Maurice*. Like Wescott, Forster had felt isolated and tormented by his homosexuality. He began the novel in 1913 under the benign influence of a gay mentor a generation older than he. Forster made a pilgrimage to the Victorian sexual radical Edward Carpenter and his working-class partner Edward Merrill, approaching the older man "as one approaches a saviour."

But Merrill had more corporeal ideas. He made a pass at the young and timid Forster—"touched my backside—gently and just above the buttocks," Forster wrote wryly decades later. "The sensation was unusual and I still remember it, as I remember the position of a long vanished tooth. It was as much psychological as physical. It seemed to go straight through the small of my back into my ideas . . . I then returned to where my mother was taking a [rest] cure, and immediately began to write *Maurice*."[2]

Forster tinkered with the novel for decades. He found excuse after excuse not to publish—first to protect his mother's feelings,

2. Ibid., 215.

then to protect Bob's. He decided finally that posthumous publication would be best. So the reading public discovered *Maurice* in 1971, two years after the Stonewall riots. But in its long unpublished private life *Maurice* became a talisman of gay friendship, a secret passed from hand to hand among a circle of intimates whom Forster trusted. Wescott was delighted to be among them.

We cannot know whether Forster understood how deeply Wescott identified with Forster and the *hegira* of writing *Maurice*. The psychological and stylistic similarities between Wescott and his mentor are striking. Like Wescott and his narrator Alwyn Tower in "A Visit to Priapus," Forster's "self-consciousness is extraordinary."[3] His sensitivity opened him to a subtle inner world—and occasionally it paralyzed his creativity. In his gay fiction, like Wescott, Forster grapples with the intricacy of intimacy, both the poisonous distortions and the creative complexity of the closet.

Wescott too agonized over his story, and refused to publish it during his lifetime. But it is a mistake merely to conflate the value of Wescott's story with the tortured circumstances of its creation. This almost-novella is a wonderful story, "an intellectual effort, a moral embrace."[4] "A Visit to Priapus" is a meditation on desire and art, a rueful, comic, brutally honest consideration of sex and its human limitations.

∽

Wendy Moffat is the author of the prize-winning *A Great Unrecorded History: A New Life of E. M. Forster* (Farrar, Straus and Giroux, 2010). She is a professor of English at Dickinson College.

3. Glenway Wescott, *A Visit to Priapus and Other Stories*, 50.
4. Ibid., 71.

Acknowledgments

Dedication to any literary work requires some sort of inspiration and encouragement because, almost always, there are obstacles, deflating discouragements, and dark days along the way. After editing Glenway Wescott's journals and stories, and researching and writing his biography, I have to acknowledge the man himself. No one ever loved literature and language more. Both Marianne Moore and Katherine Anne Porter scolded him for dedicating himself so often to the work of others. Likewise, literary editor Robert Phelps helped the elderly Wescott overcome the doubts and regrets that often haunted him. Another key figure is Anatole Pohorilenko, a faithful and thoughtful executor.

One must acknowledge the role of our great libraries in helping us put the artist's work and personal story in perspective. I am grateful to curator Timothy Young and the staff of the Beinecke Library at Yale. Thanks also to the staff of the Berg Collection of the New York Public Library.

Fate plays a role in which publisher brings a book to its readers. My thanks to acquisition editor Raphael Kadushin for his savvy decision-making, instincts, and experience. And the entire effort at the University of Wisconsin Press—editorial, production, marketing, art, and events planning—is like a throwback to the golden age of book publishing. Thanks to all.

Special thanks for great advice to three writers: San Francisco's Kevin Bentley, Toronto's Ian Young, and Wisconsin's Richard Quinney.

As Wescott readers old and new know, the spirit of Glenway dedicates this book to Monroe Wheeler.

Introduction

Glenway Wescott was a perfectionist, and that quality was both a key to his talent—as a poet turned exacting prose writer—and a handicap, because he often had trouble finishing his work. Yet what he did finish holds up: novels, stories, essays, plus two books of posthumous journals revealing a life rich in literature, art, and famous friendships. But perhaps one more work—this group of previously uncollected stories—can reveal even more about Wescott himself. The title story, unpublished in his lifetime, was called "a posthumous masterpiece" by Ned Rorem in his diaries. "A Visit to Priapus" is a long story written in 1938 about a gay liaison. Like E. M. Forster's novel *Maurice*, it was considered unpublishable at the time and for many decades afterward. Now it appears here, surrounded by other autobiographical stories—several also never previously published. Together they form a truthful, chronological portrait of the author.

For those unfamiliar with the author, Glenway Wescott (1901–87) went from living on a poor Wisconsin farm to accepting a University of Chicago scholarship when he was only sixteen, but his education was cut short after three semesters by a near-fatal case of the Spanish Flu. Still, he became known among the Imagist poets, and his lyrical novel of Wisconsin, *The Apple of the Eye* (1924), was very well received. His lifelong partner, Monroe Wheeler, convinced Wescott to move first to New York, then to France to live among the expatriates. There he achieved fame with *The Grandmothers* (1927), a best-selling chronicle-style novel of the Midwest. His Midwestern fiction ended with a book of stories, *Goodbye, Wisconsin* (1928), and a deluxe encased story, "The Babe's Bed" (1930). A book of prewar essays, *Fear and Trembling* (1932), missed its mark (prophetic but too indirect and elegant), and *A Calendar of Saints for Unbelievers* the same year was witty and comical but a small work.

Back in America in the 1930s, Wescott was frustrated after two abandoned novels. Meanwhile, Monroe Wheeler began his long career as director of publications and (later) exhibitions at New York's Museum of Modern Art, and their co-resident companion, George Platt Lynes, soon made his name as a photographer. However, by 1938 Wescott found his narrative voice with several stories, including "Priapus." He would not publish that story in his lifetime, but it led directly to perhaps his greatest achievement, the novella *The Pilgrim Hawk* (1940)—"among the treasures of twentieth-century American literature," wrote Susan Sontag. There would be a Book-of-the-Month-Club best seller set in World War II, *Apartment in Athens* (1945), as well as a few more abandoned novels. After that, Wescott turned to essays—including the volume *Images of Truth* (1962)—reviews, and his journals. Because his brother Lloyd married the heiress and art patron Barbara Harrison (they appear under fictitious names in two stories in this collection), Glenway had a home on their western New Jersey farm, in addition to Monroe Wheeler's city apartment. While he had two best sellers during his long life, he mostly lived a comfortable but near penniless life, "a bird in a golden cage," as he said.

Over the decades, Wescott forgot about "A Visit to Priapus." He remembered that, early on, artist Paul Cadmus and other friends admired it. But the subject matter of explicit homosexuality doomed it to his abandoned projects. In the 1960s, when freelance editor Robert Phelps began editing Wescott's early journals, Glenway pulled a copy of the long story from his massive set of papers. Thinking it a failure, he asked if Phelps could salvage some bits and pieces for the journals. A day later Phelps phoned in "almost hysterical admiration," seeing the connection between "Priapus" and *The Pilgrim Hawk*.

Yet even in the post-Stonewall years, when Wescott believed in it once again, the story remained unpublished. That was ironic because it was Wescott and Christopher Isherwood who arranged the publication of E. M. Forster's long-suppressed *Maurice* in 1971. Wescott spoke about getting "Priapus" published as a little deluxe book in Europe during his final years, but it never happened.

After minimal light editing by me (picking the most Wescott-like adjectives where he left choices), a private chapbook was printed in 1995, just as a reading copy. "A Visit to Priapus" was included in a big British anthology, *The New Penguin Book of Gay Short Stories* (2003) edited by David Leavitt and Mark Mitchell, but in America it appeared only in the short-lived small journal *Ganymede* (2009, no. 3), thanks to the late, literature-loving publisher John Stahle. Even most Wescott readers have never seen it, until now.

The real-life autobiographical story is simple enough. Glenway and Monroe lived with George Platt Lynes as a threesome, but the intimacy was mostly between Monroe and George. Frustrated with his love life and his writing, Wescott took up a friend's suggestion that he take a weekend trip to Maine to visit a young aspiring artist who was better known for his large endowment than for his canvases. In the story, Wescott's familiar fictional self, Alwyn Tower, is a writer absorbed with concerns of love and lust and art. He meets the artist, who lives a middle-class, closeted life in a small New England town. The setup is perfect for Wescott's first-person account as well as his interior sort of writing. What follows is a long day, a sleepless sexual night, and the morning after. Through it all his character describes this misadventure beautifully, and thinks of his life and his loves at home, and finally reflects on the good that sex can do, even in somewhat ridiculous circumstances. It's perfect subject matter for Wescott, who was a close friend of Dr. Alfred Kinsey, the famous sex researcher. As is often the case with his best writing, there is much more to the story than the plot.

The first of these autobiographical stories, "Adolescence," actually did appear in the 1928 collection *Goodbye, Wisconsin*, but it is essential for the present work. In the story thirteen-year-old Philip goes to a Halloween party dressed as a girl at the suggestion of his fifteen-year-old friend Carl. In real life, young Glenway was in a relationship with a boy named Earl who had not yet discovered girls. Wescott once noted in a book inscription that in 1914 he stayed overnight in West Bend "in order to go to this party disguised as a girl. I was thirteen; 'Carl' was fifteen."

Published in *Harper's Magazine*, "Mr. Auerbach in Paris" is based on his first visit to Paris in the early 1920s, when he was working as a secretary to a rich philanthropist, Henry Goldman. It not only describes his wonderful first impressions of Paris, it reveals a chilling truth from the past—that many well-meaning powerful people in America and England totally misunderstood the soaring nationalism in Germany. Then there is "The Babe's Bed," which was published only as a little encased deluxe book in 1930. Alwyn Tower / Wescott is an expatriate writer leaving the luxury of Paris to visit his poor family in Wisconsin during the Depression. The family tensions remind the adult narrator of his boyhood and the fierce battles he had with his father in childhood—not unusual with young males but all too familiar to the gay male in an unsupportive home.

Next is "A Visit to Priapus," which has waited all these years for its readers. Also written in the same time period is the never-before-published "The Stallions," which reminds us that Wescott did live most of his days at the large farm of his brother and sister-in-law. When his character mentions that he's never seen horses breeding, his brother "Tim" arranges that he witness two pairs of horses mating. Only Wescott could bring such elegant prose to such subject matter. Over the years, even decades later, he kept returning to this material to add human stories about country life, to build "The Stallions" into something much larger. He was frustrated in trying to expand this story into a novella because the additional drafts are good but unfinished, and would require major editing. Yet the original material, covering only the horse breeding scenes, remains sharp and clear in finished typescript, and it belongs here.

When Wescott made a prewar trip to Paris in 1938 it left impressions that became "The Frenchman Six Feet Three," which appeared in *Harper's Magazine* in 1942. Once more, the narrator is the fictional Wescott, Alwyn Tower. The Frenchman named Roger is based on Michel Girard, a young friend from Jean Cocteau's circle. Michel's constant friend Alain is obviously his companion. A member of the army reserve, Roger is equipped with a uniform too small for his large frame, symbolic of how France was unprepared for war. An American journalist in the story, Linda Brewer, is closely drawn from Wescott's lifelong friend, the *New Yorker* Paris correspondent Janet Flanner. Wescott left notations to confirm the identities. Interestingly, Linda's/Janet's companion in the story, Mrs. Lavery, is based on neither of Flanner's longtime lovers, Solita Solano and Natalia Danesi Murray. Instead, Mrs. Lavery is based on Flanner's short-term lover Noel Haskins Murphy, a professional singer, as the story notes. Even such small footnotes of gay history are fascinating to uncover after seventy years. This story provides a vivid, unrushed, highly detailed look at prewar Europe, which is very interesting in light of Wescott's World War II novel that followed in three years, *Apartment in Athens* (translated into seven languages, and now a foreign film, *Appartamento ad Atene*).

There is only a paper-thin difference between Wescott's first-person stories and first-person essays. Considering that the theme in this collection is truthful autobiography, it seems permissible that a few of these stories were written as essays. In fact, this seems to matter even less in our current literary age where twenty-five-year-olds write fictionalized "memoirs" with composite characters and events. "The Love of New York," which appeared in *Harper's Bazaar*, has a rare charm because, much as Glenway loved farmland and nature, it describes the Manhattan he loved in the 1940s, during the war years, a rich cityscape that is partly still familiar and partly lost in time. And he candidly sees himself in that experience; a revealing mini-portrait of himself.

"An Example of Suicide" is another story that was never-before published and is based on a sensational news event of July 27, 1938. A young bank clerk named John W. Warde stood on a ledge of the Hotel Gotham (now the Peninsula Hotel) threatening to jump, from 11:40 a.m. to 10:38 p.m., while thousands watched and jeered, and traffic stopped. At the time, all the newspapers and picture magazines covered it in depth. Of course Wescott's perspective is more complex and analytical. His narrator leaves the daytime scene in the street to go to the apartment of the male "friend with whom I live." He considers in great detail the young man's plight, and how most of us are capable of such despair, but don't surrender to it. However, he realizes, the bluff of suicide could cause a proud male to go through with it. Presently, the character that is Monroe Wheeler comes home and comments on the dramatic standoff. Finally at midnight some young friends visit with the news of the sad ending. Wescott fills in the after-story. Following the widespread journalistic coverage, "An Example of Suicide" was an unusual story to place. One literary magazine held it for months and politely declined, and the clean typescript became buried in the Wescott Papers. It is chilling to note that on August 9, 2012, a man jumped from the twenty-second-floor sun deck of the same hotel, and the next day's newspaper photos showed only one terrace below that, the seventeenth floor ledge from which John Warde had jumped.

Of the main selections, the last, "The Odor of Rosemary," is actually a perfectly contained story which is the second half of a long essay that appeared in the journal *Prose* in 1971. Wescott's late personal essays are beautiful; they can meander like a winding walkway but always skillfully take you back to his main point and moral. The first half of "The Odor of Rosemary" is like that, but suddenly the second half becomes the compassionate story included here. The elder Wescott, in his best form at seventy, looks back on a 1935 ocean voyage, marked by the scent of the herb rosemary from the coast of Spain, when he befriends a melancholy young man from California and learns of his sorrows.

The appendix includes two essays and an unpublished, adolescent experimental story. The first essay, "The Valley Submerged," appeared in the *Southern Review* in the summer of 1965. It mixes his thoughts about the late-1950s flooding of his country home and valley to create a reservoir, and the 1950s Cold War fears. However, at age 77 Wescott handwrote a copy of "The Valley Submerged" and included several late comments and observations. That is the version presented here. The next piece, "A Call on Colette and Goudeket," appeared first in *Town and Country* in January 1953, and then in his book of literary reminiscences, *Images of Truth* (1962). It gives the reader a view of Wescott's love of and devotion to literature, which also was clear in his decades of work for the American Academy of Arts and Letters. He first met Colette in 1935 when he served as a translator during her American publicity tour. He later wrote the long introduction to *The Short Novels of Colette* (1951). But this little piece is about a visit to Colette and her companion when she was bedridden in Paris in 1952. As for the never-before-published 1923 experimental story, "Sacre de Printemps"—influenced by Mary Butts in a surrealist style—it stands totally outside the artistic scope of the rest of his lifelong prose, but is offered here as an interesting read. It is based on twenty-two-year-old Glenway's visit to a young American gay couple in England, at Oxford, during the same trip that would provide the material for "Mr. Auerbach in Paris." The kaleidoscopic images are poetic but abstract and difficult. However, the dialogue reveals vivid glimpses of 1923, such as a young Sinn Fein member who mentions "a boy I loved" killed in the Irish uprising, and some first impressions of James Joyce's *Ulysses* ("Marion" is Molly Bloom). It has little to do with his life work, but it has historical importance—written a decade before Charles Henri Ford and Parker Tyler's controversial, surrealistic, homophile novel, *The Young and Evil*.

These stories may be appreciated by different readers in different ways, but all, I believe, with pleasure.

A Visit to Priapus and Other Stories

Adolescence

In the attic bedroom of a large house at twilight two youngsters were trying to make up their minds about a masquerade party. Out of the stairway rose an agreeable odor of bath-towels and tobacco and face-powder, reminding the younger boy of his friend's brothers and fashionable mother, whom he admired but who often embarrassed him. He came from the country, and was sensuous and timid.

Carl, who was at home there, was the youngest of the four sons of one of three brothers who owned the flour-mill and several stores and a number of houses in the town. Philip had only his father and mother, and they were poor. They were respectively fifteen and thirteen years old.

Both were excited by the illicit cigarette which Carl was holding outside the dormer window. Past his friend's face, whose cynical expression was meant to reveal and in fact greatly exaggerated the effect of the smoke, Philip gazed down into the quiet though populous twilight, leaf-green and pink. The small town rose from the river-bed on a number of overlapping hills; heaped with branches and evening silhouettes, the light color of the buildings died down.

It was from the bulky yellow house under the elms that they had received an invitation to a fancy-dress party. A girl named Rita who went to school with them lived there; she was going to be fifteen years old. They could not make up their minds what disguises to adopt. Philip's imagination ran to lace curtains and borrowed jewelry, but it was Carl who said: "I'll tell you what. You dress up as a woman. I'll get my brother's glee club suit and wear a mustache. We're supposed to wear masks, anyway, and they won't know you and I'll say you're my cousin from Milwaukee. You'll make quite a pretty girl. Just for the fun of it. See what it's like."

The next afternoon they asked his cousins Lucy and Lois in the house next door to help them. These two lovely sisters lived with their aged stepmother and a maiden aunt. Men of their age at once unmarried and worth marrying almost never appeared on the scene of the small town; they were clairvoyant and knew what to expect; so in spite of their fresh bodies and liquid eyes they already had the serene manners of sisters of charity. They were working at a frock for someone else; eyelet embroidery and ribbons and batiste lay in disorder on the polished table.

As Carl explained what they wanted he leaned against the mantelpiece sturdily, in imitation of his elder brothers giving orders to indulgent women. "You'll find him a dress, won't you? You have a lot of old stuff in the cherry cupboard."

The young women were charmed by the plan. Though Philip wanted to keep even his unspoken requests within modest bounds, he could not keep his poor farmer-boy's gaze from the rich work-table: the blueprint patterns, the bolt of white cloth like a flattened pilaster, the chiseled pleats, the squares cut out—transparent marble of some fresh and incomplete and ethereal architecture into which a chilly bare body could slip as into a dwelling . . .

He came there again two days later to be tormented by one of the worst forms of fatigue, that of erect immobility touched by many nervous hands, pinched and patient, measured, turned about, discussed, labored over. They stood him on a stool by way of a pedestal. The sharp mouths of two pairs of scissors played about him, as well as a quiverful of pins both black and nickel-plated, often piercing to the skin. He was as happy and nervous as a young martyr.

The excitement of the sisters increased as they worked. Out of some bright old rags, pins, coral beads, and a boy—a farm boy at that—they were creating a woman's charm. It might have been a symbolical doll that they were dressing, to attract, by some rule of magic, out of the sluggish village to themselves, a multiple and passionate attention: rude young beaux dangerously troubled in the dim bowling alley, gray-haired lawyers and doctors stealing across the lawn with gifts, perfect husbands chosen finally after the most luxurious hesitations, coming there by appointment to carry them off . . . Their rather young faces of spinsters by accident grew still younger, the pure mouths and the pinched nostrils animated by laughter, imagination, sighs.

Disturbed by this hilarity in the decorous house, their old maiden aunt came to the head of the stairs and called down, "What is the matter?"

Even Carl, comparatively useless and at ease like a proprietor, regarded his cousins with a new interest and wondered at the indifference of his brothers who were old enough to fall in love with them. When they were silent and busy their mouths remained slightly open, as if the invisible forms of the tones of their voices stayed on their lips. Because of them he began to feel the approach of a certain excitement in the night before him: a tumult of masked girls, lawns resilient under fleeing and pursuing feet, games which would be only a pretext for taking almost painful kisses and for laughing at them once taken—the approach of a sweet disorder in which he was very likely to forget his less and less recognizable friend.

The work was done. The sisters and Carl led the bedizened youngster into another room to a tall mirror. He wore an old-rose satin dancing frock, and long kid gloves, and on his head a black velvet picture hat out of which there pressed against the nape of his neck and his temples one of the blond wigs which the maiden aunt had worn before she had felt obliged to change to gray, unpleasantly soft and audible, sweet with cologne-water. The full skirt had been tucked up behind so that it resembled the tumbled plumage of some lean, pink swan; and out of the square bodice rose his unfamiliar throat powdered and wound with coral.

"I declare, he is prettier than any girl in the village," Lucy cried.

But during the vigorous remodeling which the dress had received at the sisters' hands, the enervate satin had lost the last of its freshness; the worn ruffles and the pulled seams held together with a bedraggled tenacity; the fairy-tale pink was veined with mauve. Philip's extreme youth of a boy made a woman's maturity; and in the mirror his face had the frightened expression of a woman who feels that she is too gaudily, too youthfully dressed for her age.

Over his puckered sleeves the sisters, radiant and amused, were looking; and between their faces in the mirror Carl's face, which astonished him. How could Carl's appearance be changed by his metamorphosis—or was he merely seeing him with the eyes of the part he was dressed to play? Smaller than before, hardy and provocative, masculine to an enigmatic degree, smiling a humorless, drowsy smile . . . The disguised boy met the other's glance, and thinking himself the cause of the equivocal expression, blushed.

Lois and Lucy said wistfully, "Have a good time," and said goodbye.

Together the boys crossed the adjoining lawn toward Carl's home. Philip was anxious on all occasions; in this preposterous costume, if he went into the house, he was certain to be teased unmercifully by Carl's brother; so he resigned himself to going without any supper.

There was a great maple tree on the lawn, inside which, on the lower limbs, the brothers had built a platform. Carl threw his arms around his friend's rustling knees and lifted him as high as he could. Philip caught a branch and carefully pulled himself up into the hiding-place.

"If you were a girl you'd gather your skirts together," Carl said. Then he hurried indoors to dine and put on his evening clothes and false mustache.

The sun had set; there would be no moon that night, so it must have been the earth which filled the sky with overtones of foliage and with the pearls of its pale buildings and pale fields. Inside the tree everything was dim and still. The platform on which Philip sat was enclosed by the light-colored, slim, wayward pillars of the branches.

He could smell the food being served inside the house; that was the first penalty of his adventure; he began to feel that it would not be the last. Ants went up and down the branches of the tree; he kept watch that none should get into his flounces. This led him to try to feel his boy's body inside them; he shook himself from head to toe, and decided that wearing women's clothes was like being tucked into a luxurious, portable bed. A whalebone in the old corset hurt him and had to be pushed back into place.

He listened to bicycles going down the streets and the discords of the different kinds of bells all over the town. Then he heard something else, this time on the lawn below, and hunted for it through the foliage. It was Carl's eldest brother, admirable, somber, and hurried. Philip shrank out of sight.

He was too young to find anything worth thinking about under such abnormal circumstances; so he let his imagination drift heedlessly, forgetful both of the nonexistent cousin from Milwaukee whom he was supposed to represent and the gallant widow, desperately eager to please, in weakened frills, whom in fact he did resemble.

Carl came back and climbed up in the tree until it should be time to go to the party. He brought the hungry masquerader some sandwiches and a bottle of root-beer. He lit a match, for it was almost dark, a flickering light among the dark, flickering leaves; and each adding to the somewhat exalted notion he had of his own appearance the comical image of the other, they laughed a little. Then they sat quietly and talked.

In spite of the difference in their ages they had entered high school together the September before, Philip coming from the farm to do so. The boys Carl had grown up with had been greatly inclined to bully the new, somewhat effeminate, rustic boy; Carl had defended him. In return, by the usual frauds, Philip had lightened for him the burdens of getting an education. On this basis they had become inseparable companions.

Philip's gratitude for being championed was flattering. In a childish way he was eccentric, which contrasted well with his friend's ideal banality, and his unpopularity satisfied in his friend rudiments of jealousy. He lacked common sense and offered instead the poetry of being surprised and being excited in all his five senses by everything and easily hurt. On the whole, Carl enjoyed in him qualities that he would later enjoy in women.

Outside the tree the swallows wheeled up and down, chattering, in front of the evening star.

The girl to whose fifteenth birthday party they were going might not have invited the new boy from the country, had she not had a weakness for Carl ever since an intimate summer afternoon in a forest when they were children. She wished to flatter him by acknowledging his right to be followed wherever he went by his small protégé. Up in the tree Carl told Philip about that afternoon.

Philip, on the other hand, would not have had the courage to go, but for Carl's insistence and the promise of protection which it implied. The latter, a little boastful about his knowledge of the world, replied to every expression of curiosity on his friend's part by a recommendation of actual experience. Philip had often asked what happened at parties in the village.

Giving anxious attention to his false mustache, Carl smoked another forbidden cigarette.

For several years Philip had had a constant sense of growing up; it was less a sense than a sensation, as if he could actually feel cells expanding, new nerves winding like tendrils of a vine about certain muscles, bones hardening. Goodbye childhood; and his imagination, genuinely terror-stricken, crying to maturity—coming, coming, coming! Himself as a grown man looked forward to, cherished with vain anxiety, wondered about, feared and forecast in innumerable juvenile ways . . . Thus it was as a sort of Narcissus that he had been ready to bend selfishly, attentively, toward the mirror of the life of a somewhat older boy such as his friend. Desire for himself, his prospective self, was a large part of his affection.

His friend's house poured out upon the grass a brilliant light, but it was almost silent. Only the nurse, hopelessly in love, was singing Carl's little sister to sleep with a lullaby in which there were panting tones that Philip did not understand.

He was miserably innocent, or believed himself to be, imagining, as adolescents do, that there is more to know than there is. Up on the platform in the maple tree, in the attitude of Narcissus over the pool of darkness and grass, almost flat on his stomach in spite of his finery, he asked Carl questions about girls, hoping for answers about men—that is, about himself. Carl replied in a shrouded, muttering voice, taking advantage of his own excitement, dealing roughly with his own modesty. The questions and the answers did not quite match; one imagined that he was preparing for life, the other was getting ready to have a good time at the party . . .

Then, here and there in the town, the hour of the party struck, and they went. It was not far. Rita's house reached through the trees to meet them with its arms of light lying loose and open in the grass, its cries of rough amusement made by many young guests. They put on their two small black masks.

A dozen or more dressed-up youngsters had arrived before them, as they had hoped. Carl got through the false introduction well enough, made very polite by the danger of laughing. Philip slipped into a chair which stood by itself in one corner.

In the rather rich rooms, untidy with imitation flowers and twisted streamers, red with paper lamp-shades, there were tramps who had tin boxes of hay-leaves for tobacco, Indian chiefs thrust full of rooster feathers, a soldier in the uniform of no particular country, two girls in wall-paper, a Fairy Soap girl carrying a bunch of millinery violets, a pallid dark-haired Irish girl as an Oriental dancer. These disguises were all the prettier for being hasty and imperfect, but there would be little left of them by midnight.

Philip should have received the prize for the finest costume, if there had been one, and did receive a great deal of sidelong scrutiny. Then the games began, which he was not asked to join, and with the games the rude flirtations.

A lamp shone in his eyes, but he preferred not to move. He was too young ever to have been so lonesome before. He could not make up his mind whether the other guests had recognized him. They had not done so in the first place, while he was being introduced; that much was certain. Later, to denounce him as an imposter, they would have had to confess their original gullibility. And the revelation of his sex and identity might have made him one of them; cunningly hostile, perhaps they realized this and preferred to let him sit there—ignorant of their opinion, that is, half-ignorant of his own identity—an equivocal wallflower. Whenever two or three of them withdrew to the adjoining rooms, he imagined that the hilarity he heard concerned him; they giggled as if it were their common secret who he was—not his own. Rita, their hostess, who knew, spoke to him now and then but scarcely tried to draw him out of his corner.

Carl left him to his own resources. He was having a good time and was so excited that he did not look happy. Sometimes he gazed across the room with the strange smile which Philip remembered, which, perhaps, he had provoked, which now testified to pleasure that he certainly was not going to share.

The eagerness and the provoking mockery of the group of masked girls was concentrated on Carl. They too glanced repeatedly at the unhappy figure in the corner; and whoever they thought it was, their gaze expressed the hatred which immature girls feel for an older woman, less lovely, less ignorant, more sumptuously dressed. Defiantly, they grew less and less reserved. Carl profited by this rivalry with a symbol.

Having with the aid of his cousins made a girl out of his country friend, he seemed to have lost his awe of girls, perhaps even his respect for them. Rough and dreamy at once, he teased and touched them all; his impertinence seemed involuntary and was not shame-faced; apparently no one took offence. Something had aroused his marauding instincts of a half-grown man, quickened the progress of emotions about which, up to that night, he had done little more than talk. He himself had a look of astonishment at the liberties he was taking.

The other boys in consequence grew coarser in their speech and gestures, hoping, if not to outdo him, to check his triumph by embarrassing the girls. In their turn they looked boldly across the room at his supposed cousin from Milwaukee, perhaps thinking of revenge; but not one had the courage to sit down in the conspicuous corner.

Rita's mother, with great complacence, had begged them to have a good time and not to break anything, and retired to her bedroom.

The games were lively but not quite amusing. A ring on a string brought the slightly scarred and stained boys' hands into contact with smaller moist hands and even among the folds of disheveled costumes. Humiliating positions and red-faced kisses were assigned as forfeits. A girl played the piano, but not many of them knew how to dance, and these seemed unhappy to be in each other's arms under the eyes of their friends. Then chairs were placed in a row, around which they marched; the music stopped and started without warning, and they scrambled for seats; there were pushes and pinching and needless collisions. Sometimes one or two would pause by the dining-room door to stare at the pitchers of lemonade, the plates of sandwiches and cake covered with napkins; but Rita did not want to serve the refreshments too soon, lest the party come to an end.

One of the Indians and the girl with a bunch of violets moved chairs into Philip's corner, one on each side of him. They found nothing to say. The girl's look of languid interrogation shifted from her partner to the disguised boy and back again. The Indian pulled his fingers. Then the girl rose and darted out on the porch. Glancing back at Philip with an indefinable expression, the sturdy youth followed. Through the bay window Philip saw a single shadow made of both their figures, and supposed it was a kiss.

The party could not go on much longer in those small warm rooms. An increasing impatience for the dark and the bushes, for long grass in which footsteps would be lost, for soft boughs lost in the sky, was revealed by everyone's glances toward the doors and windows.

Carl pursued his Irish-Turkish girl from one chair or sofa to another with boisterous but somber violence. Philip waited until they reached the opposite corner of the other room, and then slipped into the hall. No one was there; the door stood open and the freshness of cut grass and blossoming syringas drifted in. He wanted to go out on the porch, but did not dare, because of the sweethearts who had just left him. He sat down a little way up the stairs, took off his gloves and his half-mask, rested his overladen woman's head in the palms of his boy's hands . . .

He was not alone many minutes. The boy in the uniform of no particular country followed him. Neither knew what to say; the soldier sat down on the same step. Philip knew him by sight—his father was a carpenter, his name was Art Sampson. He supposed he must have figured out his identity. Then Art Sampson took his hand and put one arm around him. Philip twisted about in confusion and changed his mind—obviously the soldier did not know who he was. He tried to get up, but one foot somehow caught in the skirt and he was afraid of tearing it. The soldier sighed with his lips pursed. Philip did not know what to do. "Give me a kiss," the other muttered. The kiss slipped off Philip's cheek into the scented strands of his wig. He got away, giving the soldier a kick, leaving him to his astonishment. The kick hurt his own foot because Lucy's slippers were so thin. He came back into the sitting room alone.

Not many of the guests were there. They had gone out by a door which opened directly on the porch. Carl was gone. Two unattractive girls on a sofa were telling secrets. Some boys were playing poker on the floor; paper flowers and streamers lay all about them, crumpled and untwisted. The remaining costumes were also torn and trodden upon. Philip stood there, miserably excited.

Out in the dark, as usual, couples mixed up with the time of night and the porches and the flowering shrubs, one girl laughing under a tree with a shrouded sound (a hard hand was over her mouth), someone trying to play a stringed instrument, secrets being told and being felt, no more misery in the kisses, no more self-consciousness in such games as were being played . . . Carl was there with his Irish friend.

Everyone had forgotten Philip; he might as well not have come. He could not make up his mind where to sit down. His dress hung askew; he straightened it with boyish jerks under which the corrupted silk gave way. Their hostess, Rita, dressed as a queen, was sitting loosely on a sofa; the other Indian, a slow fellow, held her hand and seemed to be studying it. She looked feverish and disappointed.

Philip decided to go home, and wondered why he had not done so before. He did not want to say goodbye or see the boy in the hall again. So he slipped into the dining room as if to look at the refreshments, thence into the kitchen, from the back porch to the pitch-dark alley, and down the alley to the street.

There he felt frightened for a few moments. Men might be coming home from the saloons, the billiard parlor; some of them were capable of anything; they would think the worst of a woman alone at that hour, in such clothes, and tear off the clothes if he told them who he was. He walked as fast as he could. A boy's stride went badly in Lucy's shoes. He stumbled over the dress and tore it. Now he did not mind taking it back to the sisters in bad condition. He would tell them, he thought vindictively, that he had not had a good time—they would be sorry.

The wide sky, he saw, was dappled with stars. He was angry as well as tired. Carl had played a trick on him, neglected him, deserted him. He did not know whether that would bring an end to their friendship or make it more substantial, equalize it. He would make another friend if this one failed . . .

Under the street lights the lawns foamed with flowering plants. From Rita's back door he had turned down a side-street to avoid passing her garden, and he did not see anybody in the others.

Perhaps if he had talked to the pseudo-soldier they would have made friends, and laughed at the fraud of the one, the error of the other. Soon he would be enough older for there to be no more disguises, nor need to be taken care of, nor harm in being neglected. He hated women's clothes; by a deliberate step he tore the ruffled skirt again.

Out of the evening's misery in retrospect faded all willingness to be unhappy. The only good time had been up in the tree at twilight, the pink satin amid the green leaves forming a world of their own, without excitement or humiliation; then being disguised as a woman had been like being a large flustered bird guarded by the branches. How long ago—it might have been sometime in his childhood. Never, he resolved, would he have such fairy-tale ideas again.

He had to cross the river on a little echoing foot-bridge to get to the part of town in which he lived. An odor similar to that of cucumbers rose from the water and the mud. There down below the brown currents were trickling, the green willows with gentle boughs caressing themselves. He no longer envied the caresses in Rita's garden. He was sick of the age he had been too long, the age of envy and masquerades, of petty martyrdoms which have a savor of joy, when nothing is satisfactory in solitude; and tried not to think that some of this youthfulness might be natural to himself and so permanent, for he wanted that night to mark plainly an end . . .

There was no one on Main Street. The pool room and bowling-alleys were closed. He made up his mind to go into one of these places as soon as he could save money from the small allowance which his parents gave him and get someone to teach him to play. He had looked through the windows often enough to know what they were like. The air marbled the smoke, the broad green tables under the light bulbs shaded with green glass swinging gently, the smooth cues manipulated according to complex rules, the ivories rolling, twirling, meeting, hard cheek to cheek, with a little pure click, the men in shirt-sleeves, absent-minded, vain, and skillful; and down below in the basement the alleys of glimmering wood, waxed and exquisitely jointed, stretching away under the great growling balls to the pins in perfect order, and the only Negro in the town to set them up when they fell, his ugly face shining . . . Philip smiled for the first time since he had been dressed up in these rustling torn clothes. He was too young to be strong; he might never have brutal strength or direct, effective desires; he believed that he could be skillful.

He wished that he had a luxurious house like Carl's at the other end of town to go home to—the odor of bath-towels and tobacco mounting the wide staircase with classic banisters; and the luxury he wished for was something serviceable and severe like the felt and ivory and the waxed wood behind the shabby facades on Main Street. He wished that he had a rich mother like Carl's to satisfy once and for all his desire for such things as the satin clothing and soft foliage, in the maple tree after sunset; and robust, indifferent brothers, not to protect him but to be imitated by him. Instead it was to Mrs. Dewey's boarding-house that he was making his way as fast as he could.

He opened the door cautiously. The dirty stairs were lit by a gas-jet. The room in which Mrs. Dewey slept opened off the first landing. She called, "Who's that?" He did not answer, but mounted more quietly. By a creaking of the boards inside her door he understood that she was looking through the keyhole. She would think that one of her other boarders, the undertaker's assistant or the patent-medicine vendor, was receiving company in the night.

Mr. Auerbach in Paris

Almost everyone felt a greatness of some kind about old Mr. Auerbach; the feeling did not derive from his appearance. Little by little he was going blind, and his eyes, under the necessary lenses of magnifying glass, were unattractive. He had a roly-poly neck, the nape of it strewn a little with snow-white hairs. His lips pouted with no definite shape. All his features were large in proportion to the physiognomical area they occupied. It was an expressive face, waxing with enthusiasm, waning with worry; but in the least emotion, even happiness, he looked as if on the verge of tears, which in one whom you knew to be a man of power seemed absurd.

But no matter; if you could not see you could sense that he was shrewd and honorable in business, and very strict in the more intimate aspects of morality, charitable, intellectual, and art-loving. He was a millionaire retired from a great career of finance management and speculation. In the philanthropies of the ordinary sort he was not only generous but painstaking; yet it was a poor substitute for the big business he had given up. He had also occupied himself acquiring a fine collection of paintings by old masters, working hard at it. But still he had time on his hands, money to spare, and superfluous energy; which made the loss of his eyesight especially hard for him.

One whole year in my young manhood I was employed by him. At the start I had only to read aloud while he ate breakfast and before dinner, and occasionally, for two or three hours after dinner. Certain English and German newspapers interested him, as well as the *Times* and the *Sun*. I knew how to pronounce German and gradually learned what the recurrent words meant. In the evening we concentrated upon highbrow books: biographies, histories or art, and essays.

We read, I remember, an essay entitled "Leisure and Mechanism" by Bertrand Russell, the point of which was that it is better to do nothing and amount to nothing than to do a wrong thing. To make clear what this meant the noble author cited a certain newspaper-magnate who had no vices and slaved away faithfully at his lifework; and, year in and year out, for millions of newspaper readers, set the vulgarest example and advocated entirely evil policies. It would have been better for the world if he had lain snoozing on a miserable sofa or under a shade tree all his life, the philosopher said. The effect of his virtue and industriousness had been only to increase the harm he was in a position to do.

This essay infuriated Mr. Auerbach. He arose and strode around and shook his fist. He had respected Russell as a master-mathematician and admired him as a great liberal and pacifist, but this was the limit! With his most tearful look, shaking his forefinger at me, he maintained that work, hard work, no matter what hard work, was all-essential. It was a good thing in itself, indeed it was the basis of morality. Save for the necessity of it, with the sting of poverty in the lives of the poor and the desire of rich men to get richer, all men would lapse into themselves in drunkenness, lewdness, and every vile, selfish habit, he said. This righteous wrath was my introduction to a form of puritanism which is an important problem today, pro or con. In Mr. Auerbach's case it was not connected with any religion, although there was an echo of Elijah or Jeremiah in the tone of his remarks. After this he would not hear another word by Bertrand Russell and often referred to him as frivolous and a bad influence on young people.

Now and then he told me what I wanted to know about himself. Like many German-Jews in those days he was romantically pro-German. Born in the United States, the son of an old-fashioned, comfortable banking family, he was sent for higher education to Heidelberg and he never got over it. Our involvement in the so-called World War struck him as a wicked mistake; and after quarrelling with certain relatives and business associates he retired from the firm he had founded, and suffered in silence while Germany was being defeated. Even the charities of wartime were against his principles; and it was then, in the sudden loneliness of his rich Park Avenue apartment, that he was inspired to take up art collecting.

In the spring I accompanied him and his wife abroad in a half-secretarial, half-filial capacity, chiefly to keep him company when she was engaged and to give him my arm at street corners where his failing eyesight was not to be trusted. He took a last look at the museums of Europe through great binoculars, focusing them as close as he could get to one painting after another; and he added a few final treasures to his collection.

Since the War his dearest philanthropy had been assisting the German universities to re-equip their laboratories and to bring their libraries back up to date; and he had to see people in Berlin and Munich about all this, and some very distinguished sociability went with it. Even in England he found a way to be serviceable to the Fatherland, in the correction of prejudices left over from the conflict and its vindication in the eyes of the world. That was in 1923. There was a group of Englishmen just then, half in and half out of government, whose international policy and attitude toward the erstwhile enemy suited him. They were idealists, pacifists, and radical economists, and various liberal gentlemen who simply admired Germany, in its national temperament and culture and political philosophy as it appeared then, more than they admired their own nation or its allies.

Three or four were rather famous figures in 1923; today they have been forgotten. I think that we should be reminded of them and when peace is declared again ponder their example and strange influence. They founded something called the Union of Democratic Control, and they constituted what we should call a brain trust round Ramsay MacDonald while he reversed the foreign policy of Great Britain and abandoned so large a part of its military and naval power. To familiarize the general public with their principles they had a magazine, and it was in this particular that Mr. Auerbach could help them—he defrayed a part of the expense of publishing it.

As Mr. Auerbach's seeing eye and strong right arm, I had the privilege of meeting these influential men. Their aristocracy and refinement of manner and general culture were astonishing to me. Certainly the several politicians whom I had encountered in the United States were not in a class with them. And they were far from the phlegmatic type of Britisher; they expressed their gratitude to Mr. Auerbach over and again, and indeed our impression was that they would have been glad of his company even if he had not entered into their plans for the peace of Europe.

Perhaps I have not given enough emphasis to the fact that Mr. Auerbach was a very good companion; a really civilized, knowledgeable old man. It was extraordinary, given the narrow range of his life as a whole and the complacency that as a rule develops with the making of a fortune. For almost half a century his days had been spent in Wall Street, in intense concern with money matters. He once confided to me that in his waking hours, until the hateful war left him to his own devices, business had never been out of his mind for more than ten or fifteen minutes at a time; even his beloved beautiful wife had not distracted him from it. Yet now in his old age he had some grasp of all the main features of culture as such, and a personal point of view about it all. A love and a knowledge of music had come to him from his family, and having begun to buy art, he had mastered the essential facts about that also. On his brief annual holidays abroad he had kept in touch with all sorts of Europeans, and he appreciated the best in England and France and Italy as well as in Germany. He had a host of appreciative friends in New York, though not much intimacy with them; and even those who kept a bitter memory of his lack of patriotism in 1917 admired the dignified way he bore the onus of it. He had an odd, superior, deceptively simple nature. To me he was almost a hero in spite of the fact that I was to some extent, you might say, his valet.

From London we journeyed across to Paris. It was April; the French spring came early that year. It was my first trip to Paris, I was young, I had never loved a city before, of course I loved it. The famous festive style and modest proportions of its architecture surprised me as much as they pleased me; all so pale, with a rosy tinge early in the day and a blue tinge later. The beauty of Paris is too well known to write about, although naturally now it is being forgotten. The weather that week was enchanting; the sunshine rippled over everything and at the same time the moisture in the air veiled it. Those old-fashioned carpets of flowers were brought from the greenhouses and laid down amid the Tuileries and the rectangle of the Louvre and elsewhere—extremely neat patterns in the fragrant, soft cross-stitch of all the petals. The mild breezes in a few days wore them out, until the greenish and brownish warp appeared; then overnight those patterns would be gathered up and replaced with a fresh set.

Every evening we dined in the Bois; at that age I was not a gourmet, but I liked dining with fragrances and to music. What I liked best was the hush of the streets at twilight, when suddenly you were aware of the voices of the Parisians, light soprano and tenor voices, tired but complacent about the day's work, turning with their peculiar kind of gratitude to their sentiment, pleasure, and sleep.

Parisians get sleepy somewhat as birds in dusky branches do, sociably, with murmurs welcoming it. Every midnight when Mr. Auerbach retired I ran to Montparnasse, and I was almost in love with Mina Loy, the famous muse, famous there then.

One afternoon Mr. Auerbach and I came out of a great picture-dealer's in the Rue de la Paix, and turned into the Place Vendôme. He was very cheerful. We had gone to look at a little fifteenth-century Italian Madonna which, as it was described to him, he had expected to want badly; and he had been in a mixed emotion, telling himself that he ought to resist the temptation to buy it. But just now, with his binoculars on it, he had decided that it was not all it should be. This made him glad of the long time he had spent educating himself in matters of the Italian Renaissance; it had saved him money. And as he liked to feel that I was learning from him little by little, and in this issue I decidedly agreed with him, he was well disposed toward me too.

He was smoking a cigar, wielding it in his strong small fingers, often moving it from here to there across his sensitive mouth, gesturing with it and pointing with it, enjoying it. He would smoke only the choicest variety of Havana cigar, imported by him as his chief self-indulgence. We had brought along upon our journey a small trunkful of them, which was troublesome for me; at every boundary between the absurdly narrow countries I had to declare their number and value and pay duty and keep an account of it. I remember that we had a few left upon our return to New York, and I amused myself by estimating what they were worth at that point, with the accumulated assessments—a matter of several dollars each.

Mr. Auerbach liked to offer them to his friends, especially in Europe where during the War everyone had been deprived of such things. But I observed that he offered them only to the rich or the ex-rich. The poor, he assumed, would not have appreciated a blend so delicate. Even smoking, in the way his mind worked, was a thing to be made a study of, like art or like foreign affairs; and in all things the opinion of the professional and the expert was gospel. He himself smoked all day long, and Mrs. Auerbach was inclined to attribute the diminution of his eyesight to that; but she was far too sorry for him to discipline him. As diagnosed by famous oculists in Zurich and New York, the trouble was organic somehow; but for my part, thinking as usual on the basis of rash intuition, I decided that it might be mental or spiritual.

There we were, that April afternoon, strolling around the Place Vendôme, in no hurry, talking and smoking. I, in a spirit of economy, was trying to accustom myself to French cigarettes, and Mr. Auerbach jokingly promised to buy me something better; my rank little puffs beside him spoiled his fine smoke. We paused for a moment and gazed round at that small place which is (I think) the heart of Paris—that octagon of architecture standing with a strange lightness, apparently one-dimensional like a screen. I have always fancied that it could be overturned with a good hard push but that, in three centuries, no one has really touched it. Middle-class Parisians in their shabby garments with their regular steps hastened past us, preoccupied, unselfconscious, with an air of artists in their own studio; and a few upper-class Parisians and very similar foreigners went slowly into the Ritz.

The sun was shining, but so diffusely that it cast only slight shadows; the form of the Colonne Vendôme lay like a mere recollection or suggestion across the pavement. Yet it was too sunny for Mr. Auerbach; he had to shade his tragic eyes with one hand. He stood a moment in that attitude of looking at Paris; he drew a deep sigh; and he said, "I tell you, my boy, Paris is the most beautiful city in the world."

It struck me as odd and sad to hear a man who was half-blind pass judgment on the appearance of a city. But, I thought—I who had never seen this city before—what a vision of it he must have in his acquisitive mind's eye, built up at intervals in perhaps fifty years. Perhaps, I reflected, the estimation of the young, bright-eyed, unbiased observer is the least authoritative of all. Certainly I could not imagine a more beautiful city.

Mr. Auerbach sighed again. "And I tell you," he added, "it would be the greatest city in the world too if the Germans had it. What a pity they lost the War!"

I could scarcely bear to hear this, just there in the sunlight, with fine-spun shadows on the pavement, and the fragrances of tobacco and petrol and women borne round us by courteous breeze; just then, in 1923, so soon after the treaty of peace. I exclaimed, "But why, Mr. Auerbach? Why?"

You see, I was not in a position to deny what he said. I was an outsider, what you might call a virgin tourist. I was not pro-French at all, I did not know the French. On the other hand, I had spent a year in Germany and I was fond of certain Germans. There was no bias in my heart, not yet; no French fearfulness, nor even the expectation of another Armageddon. I suppose, in fact, that hearing Mr. Auerbach make that statement was the first political or historical fright of my life.

"Why, Mr. Auerbach? Why should the Germans have it?"

"Because France," he replied, "is a sensual, effeminate, idle, decadent nation. The Germans are superior to them. The Germans are a wonderful race; they are virile, hard-working, patriotic, self-sacrificing, with the future before them."

I think we never spoke of it again; in any case I did not make a quarrelsome issue of it between us. It was a history lesson for me. The point of it was the extraordinary lack of foresight of so many well-meaning Germans and German-Jews, caring for nothing in the world so much as the recovery of that injured, invalid Reich which was to grow too strong for them, so soon. I have mentioned the important English believers in Germany; there were a good many of the same persuasion and influence in every country.

The scorn of Mr. Auerbach also first suggested to my immature, uninformed American mind another grave problem: the problem of the weakness of France. Evidently Great Britain and the United States have expected too much of that nation which they have loved more than any other; and now many Englishmen and Americans say of it, word for word, what Mr. Auerbach said. A better understanding of its nature and limitations, a measure of exoneration in the eyes of the world, will be one of the chief difficulties and one of the noblest aims of the peacemaking after this war. I myself think that an entirely Anglo-Saxon world, with no respect for the weak Latin nations, no interest in their grandeur of art, no confidence in their antique sagacity, would scarcely be worth living in. Both the heritage and the future expectation of humankind would be cut in half; and it would be absurd, like a world of men without women.

Mr. Auerbach did go blind, a year or so after our journey abroad together. For various reasons I did not keep up our friendship, so that I never had to sympathize with him in person concerning the fate of the Jews and those superior liberal Aryans in Germany whom he so fondly admired. I do feel a peculiar pity for men of his type who go forward in their minds to meet and indeed welcome a new violence of history with no notion that it concerns themselves and those they love. As to the relative strength of Germany and France, Mr. Auerbach did not live to see how prophetic he had been; he died in 1938.

The Babe's Bed

All summer long that country and the sky over it, if any one gaze
could have embraced it all at once, would have been said to
be silken, Roman-striped with rainbows. Hard-looking clouds and
hard rains were interspersed with choking sunshine. Prodigal
breezes brought the needed moisture, and then perversely burned
the oats and the immature corn. The continual lightning had much
in common with the wild lilies, the grass snakes. The heat smelled
like wine. Flowerbeds, green fruit, and pools, shone in abundance in
the landscape—false jewels upon plaques of wind-engraved light.
None of it, alas, was worth as much as it looked. Never were penury
and extravagance so softly fused.

Sometimes the people had drunken hopes, sometimes their
faces fell. Nature let them hunger and thirst but drenched their
bodies instead with its overflow; through the spray they could not
see clearly. Most of them led spendthrift lives now but worked
heart-breakingly as in the past. Wistful, continually seduced by
amusements, they were educated beyond their station and lived
beyond their means, buying at a premium what their comfort-bound
and debt-driven effort produced, and in the errors of love begetting
children they could ill afford. Most of the children were beautiful
and over-ambitious.

Along the cement highways, the buildings of the small town were
draped with knitted boughs. Each one was half villa, half cabin; all

in ephemeral woodwork. The porches were linked by gossiping friendliness, which ought to have encouraged moral uniformity, self-satisfaction, prudence. But the wild atmospheres of the farming country all around (the promising dawns, reptile-colored, the storms, and undulations of the sunsets) showing themselves to the young and to young couples and retired farmers, affected their emotions otherwise and excited them to every extravagance. Very clearly against all the white clapboards, in a language of flowers, a great deal about them seemed to be expressed: hollyhocks stood for their powerful hands and red faces, hydrangeas turning brown on pruned stems for anxious innocence, for optimism gradually discolored by reality.

Within one particular house, by each piece of furniture, a genteel aspiration was inexpensively represented; and since each piece had a thousand duplicates elsewhere, there was a general effect of bareness. There were two small living rooms thrown into one; three bedrooms which the beds almost filled; a bathroom (but water had to be heated on the stove and carried up); a small kitchen without a servant. Of course there were also a phonograph, a radio cabinet, a piano, a furnace, installations of gas and electricity, an automobile. There were so many doors and windows and the walls were so thin that a sigh under the roof could be heard at the front door. Here one summer long lived a mother, a father, a young daughter, another in ill health with her husband and a baby, a grown son.

The son had returned from a great distance for a holiday. He felt poor; luxury went with his way of living—by his wits—but there was nothing left over. His relatives were genuinely poor, and childlike about it. Their frugality seemed to him sordid, their impracticality spellbound. Their unwise luxuries shocked him; important depravations they had to suffer made him ashamed of his own far-away habits. The landscape and the jeweled weather, the family's physical beauty, their unstinted affections, contrasted intolerably with their worries. He kept imagining pleas for help which no one would have uttered in any event. Perhaps the trouble was native to the place: as a boy he also had been always in trouble, grasping and ineffectual—he might be drawn into it again. In spite of himself he dreamed of running away, once more. Gallantly, the wistful women reassured him. "Do not exaggerate," they said. "Your imagination goes too far. We are in the habit of experiencing all this, and we suffer less than you think. We have the necessary." What they had was food, lodging, love, and pathetic distractions, from day to day, from hand to mouth.

There had been some changes. The younger sister, grown tall as a goddess, blunt and sensitive—she was working now between terms of college at a humiliating job in the town. Parents suddenly seem older when they have need of one. His mother, now that the child-bearing epoch with its self-denial and solitude was over, attached importance to plebian comforts and the opinion of her neighbors. His father had no savings, was dissatisfied with his work, and being vague of intellect but powerfully imaginative, dreamed a pitiful ending, as if his life were a poem. His brother-in-law was in financial straits. His married sister was still in love but sick. Her well-cut cheeks were sallow; and seeing the penalties of love, judging that existence would be vapid without it, her short-sighted sapphire eyes had grown insufferably humble. Her infant son, less than a year old, was the first of the third generation, the reason for the hardest work, the object of the most far-reaching anxieties, and for the other son (his uncle) the object of penetrating emotion. It happened that he had no child by those he loved, nor did he know how to plan to have one.

The child seemed ideal: humanity and animality united, sim-plified almost to nothing, all the possible plays of mind with flesh—character in its first incarnation as a sort of worm. Now he lay, never still, with the motions of a sea-weed. Now disappointment possessed him, and his whole body turned red with sorrow. Now for lack of other intentions, holding on to something, he dropped his weight on his heels and sharply straightened, sprang and sprang up and down in one place. Naked and murmuring in someone's clasped hands he slipped about, revolved inside his skin if he could not do more, as a fish or eel fresh from its element might. When he slept, the dimpled body (half-naked, the smallest pearls of sweat shining a little on it) seemed to grow heavier, with the fainted look of hot-weather flowers, the classic hands wide open. If under surveillance his will-power fixed upon some forbidden goal, softly, maniacally, he would maneuver and struggle—until wearier than he, one took him elsewhere, to other stimuli. The young man's heart would be in his throat, for he knew it well, this pathos of obstinacy; it was not in his power to renounce, either.

The work of the household—badly organized, for all were distracted by tenderness and worry—turned about this proud baby. It exhausted them every day; the washing and ironing, the cooking, the heating of water and the bathing, the cleaning. Often the young mother could only give advice and look on, shamefaced; now and then she herself needed attention. The child woke at five in the morning, was fed at short intervals upon steamed vegetables, fruit, porridge, and mutton juice, as well as milk, and had to be put to sleep three times in the twenty-four hours.

The home-comer worked as best he could, chiefly as nursemaid. He fed the baby and endured his fits of temper, dressed and un-dressed him, and undertook to teach him regularity in his lower functions—the muscles and the organs so powerful in miniature, insubordinate; the sounds of sensuousness and displeasure melting into each other lightly. He bathed and powdered him; the sweet-smelling hands struck his mouth, and screams of panic broke forth if the downy head was laid too low, too near the bathwater. By the small fenced bed he kept drawing away the bottle of milk from the inattentively palpitant mouth; and only the threat of deprivation made its appetite take precedence over sleep.

If he had had a son this should and might well have been he. The questioning carriage of the long head, the mouth a little loosely pouted, the light hard eyes—they were to be seen in photographs of himself at that, indeed at any age. However, all his mother's children had looked alike, and here was more than resemblance. His character recognized itself: its outline, the tendencies, the elements. The reactions to discipline, to sensation, to boredom, were his own. In himself, also, rude and selfish vigor was offset by sensibility as defenseless as if a layer of skin were lacking. He noted (it might have been by introspection) the pitiful fury, the sudden fatigues that were like falling ill, the gentle coma after a refreshment of tears. There was the same inability to abandon an ambition, the same aptitude for enjoying others, for loving others—but in proportion to enjoyment only. They were made of the same material, by one dread prescription.

Spellbound, the bachelor felt neither monotony nor fatigue, no matter what he undertook. While the little one slept he strayed about in the others' way, or all night long tossed voluptuously on the warm mattress, with the strangest lassitude of jealousy, felicity, dread. Remembering how closely in the past he had skirted disgrace and misfortune, he feared for the child; and thus looking ahead, feared for himself too—the rest of fate. So much meaningless time had to pass; should he go, or wait here to see what ensued? Of course he could not stay very much longer; but toward himself and his distant activities, felt an indifference that was all but loss of memory. So much fantastic feeling—and he had no right to it. It was folly to fancy himself a father. For he never would have the least authority over the child's life, except by other's default. How great indeed were the chances against there being any satisfaction for either of them in this kinship: the years between the two generations; the natural jealously of his humbled brother-in-law (the child's real father); his own expectations, fastidious and maybe tyrannical; the boy's probable rebellion, when manhood came, with its need to feel unique and ungoverned in the world.

But in spite of this reasoning the possessive impulse lasted and reasoned on its own account. Perhaps he would never have any other son. Having conceived of this one as his, having found himself in one baby—perhaps he would be repelled by the fear of begetting a stranger—just as frustrated lovers often find one remembrance standing between them and all further reality. Daydreaming, he felt confused excitements of having a son but no wife, a sister but no wife and no son; and with vague ideas of incest his mind played, even ironically—the pang without the remorse, the consequence without the sin. That, indeed, was how the extreme fondness of a chaste family, forever hurting and caressing, fleeing and coming home, ought to end to be logical.

And the child's mother had been his dearest before any other was known, while they were growing up. She had been exquisite, swayed by a hint or a compliment, never for a moment unaffected by her admiration of him, all wistful adaptability. It had been a funereal flowery period. They had made music and read together, penetrated by the same dream-feeling about the future, always conscious of doom—the tears starting at the first note of one or two German songs. Protestant children, each had made an effort to please his own soul as if it had been an awful God, confusing it also with the other's, so that pity and self-pity interlaced. From time to time an illness of hers, or an operation, had pointed to the possibility of her dying. In the entire family, the imagination was always alarmed. There had been more and more panic in his tenderness; and the relation might indeed have made them both very unhappy if they had not been separated, and if in the interval she had not chosen to be happy (and unhappy) with another love. She had found her young husband, worldly if not worldly-wise. She had grown more conservative in temperament, more realistic; and her health had improved.

Now there was some distance and a great difference between the brother and sister, which they liked to think that memory bridged. He could not be sorry that her affection had become somewhat conventional, somewhat careful to resist influence; for he thought of the former poetic intimacy as a prelude, perhaps to death, though, in fact, it had not been so.

But now the apprehensive family felt that she might still die, though no one said a word. Her eyes were too radiant and she looked at them too long. She rarely grew angry; and now when it did happen, it seemed too easy to control and too impersonal. She had always had a delicate exalted manner, like that of a little countrified saint, not destined to live long; but there had been enough affection about it to charm and reassure. Now all was genuine, and at times she frightened those who remembered the dangers years before.

Her husband was one of those hesitant men who inspire and content women, often by a tonic happiness making heroines of them, often also calling for heroism, alas. He was far from powerful at making money, which in hard or extravagant times might seem the more desirable virility. It happened that his family had been more comfortable, and higher up in the world, than hers; and he had fallen in love as some spoiled princeling with a milkmaid, meaning to lift her above the mean frugalities to which she had been born, and he had fallen. Penniless even then, both the vanity and the goodness of his heart let him believe he could. And the magic facility of early marriage, so favorable to attendant illusions, let him think for a while that he was doing so. But he was very self-indulgent in innocent ways, resenting every check, and over-ambitious to establish his darling in the ease she deserved, to frame their relation with the elegances it suggested. Sometimes he felt his incompetence as if it had been an amorous infirmity, and in shame grew still more ineffectual. If ever he had looked at things at their worst, he would have been good for nothing at all. His young wife knew this, and often let him, for his own sake, pamper her; and consented to new errors in hopes that it would encourage him to redeem the old. Always a desperate optimism scattered the facts out of his mind. Pride and sensibility joined to make a coward of him. So fervently did he wish to do well that he told himself hopeful untruths, and believed those he had to tell others. Thus a net of enslaving cleverness, diminishing credit, discouragement, and debt, was spread and kept strong. They were well caught in it even before the child was born and she fell ill. Forced then to take refuge in her humble home, his affliction was complete, though courteously borne. It was sharpened by lack of sympathy for this effusive tribe, too honest, all too poetic, and too fond; and indeed their pride in good works and their intimacy were often impolite to the outsider.

Throughout this puerile but ominous comedy of hand-to-mouth living, an idyllic intercourse kept the young pair in accord. Though she had none of his illusions about their situation, she had been happier than he from the start; for love seemed to her a sufficient share of the rewards of living. He was as courteous in possession as he had been in courtship, pure in speech and idealistically jealous. No unlicensed relation could have been more poignantly imprudent than this married love, entangled with debts. It was veiled in the daytime by anxiety, and a little cold at night, as if modesty fell with the dew, but never tired. Though not independent, it was unsocial; from their hopeless juvenile embrace they looked down upon the whole world. Even his injustice and lack of scruples flattered her. Her own scruples intact, she tried to keep their relations to others honorable, but brought to the task a strengthening sense of being preferred even to honor. At times she was hard and skilful to hide his weakness, at others she confessed to the spell under which she lived and wished always to live—the petty mystery of his humanity, the ignominy of her practical fate. Now she lied for him to strangers; now became a child to her own people and looked at him and at life like a puritan judge, but loved him still.

The childbirth had been accompanied by a dull and clumsy doctor, who took the worst damages as a matter of course. Already needlessly injured, she had been allowed by this fatalist and by her husband, determined to hope for the best, to get up almost at once like a primitive wife. There had been the care of the baby and all the hard work of the small home. Stimulated by necessity and by motherhood's mystic pleasures, she had kept on without help for almost a year. The child was a strong animal, and having before his birth fattened upon her strength directly, now required in a variety of ways all that was left. It was terrible to consider: the new phoenix and the old, the new sprout hollowing out the disintegrating root. And nature, making no exceptions, visited her with its usual wonder-working fevers, to which the wounded womb responded like some unbalanced mind in which, at intervals, a flood of recollections of one past agony runs bright. And a burden as of invisible rocks had to be borne, which, as if the law of gravitation had been suspended, was heavy in every direction at once, downward, upward, sideways. Usually too enfeebled even to lift her child from his bed, and too assured of her husband's inefficacy to dream a secure upbringing for him, with or without her, she felt guilty for having had a child at all. Her equivocally sad eyes on the lively body being cared for by some-one else, gave away her secret. His birth was her crown; but she was so poor that a crown disgraced her.

One night she was able to take a walk with her brother, and they went a little way out of town, around an old mill-pond. As it happened the world that evening looked altogether reasonable, well built, neither rich nor poor. They could see across many fields and roads, where workhorses, some red with a prehistoric bearing and some dappled like phantoms, were going home, and automobiles, more numerous, were racing hither and thither with rough sighs. Around them were trees which as they walked slipped back, each at a different rate in the perspective, and otherwise moved not at all; for there was no wind. Around the trees and beyond them, around the whole, rose the air, the sky—not quite yellow, like marble but softer. The surface of the pond reflected well. Frogs lightened the silence just enough. Very near the water, they stood still on the path.

"Look at our shadows," he said. "We have two heads like playing cards, and four arms."

"Then I am the Queen of Spades and you," she said, "are the King of Hearts."

"Oh no—the Knave."

"For that matter, I guess Spades are no worse than Hearts for bringing bad luck," she said.

"Do you remember when we were children, how mother would not let us play cards, and there was only one old pack in a bureau drawer?"

"To play solitaire with when someone was sick. If you were sick you couldn't work or improve your mind, so then it wasn't a waste of time."

"How limp and black they were," the brother remembered. "I'm glad we don't know what has become of them. Each card must have been a real mausoleum of dead germs."

They started back home. All the living creatures in the world except themselves—that is, those workhorses, a pasturing mare and her foal, a small boy, a bird—seemed irresolute as the dead in heaven, where there is nothing more to be resolved.

"If I didn't love my husband I should be less of a woman but easier to take care of," she said.

"And does 'if' mean anything, if I may ask?"

"Oh, nothing. Exactly nothing."

His feeling about women always inclined him to agree with their sorrow, and so to give poor consolation. "It will come out all right," he said weakly. "Your luck will turn. I want to help."

"Listen to me. This is what I have wanted to say. I am proud that you love my son; he shall always be yours as much as you like. But you mustn't fret about me, or about any of us. As soon as I get a little stronger, I promise you that I shall go to the city and have myself put together again. Of course I need money. And I need you. But you must clear out. You are too sad by nature to stand it. You have done your share. Rather, I should say, you haven't any share in this at all. I know you must have trouble enough somewhere else, all your own. This can't be yours. For the trouble is always where the joy is, and your joy is not here. There isn't any here for you."

Thus she took the child away the moment after she had given it to him in so many words. It was a great relief and a disappointment—the almost impossible, all too human burden which did him honor and made him less anomalous in his good fortune, slipping out of his arms. To the same degree that he shrank from any excess of responsibility, he always sought to prove himself able to assume it. In nature, he thought, such things balance better. Tall and attenuated shadows held up the sky; now and then another star came out, and, just enough to support its weight, the shadows darkened. They turned back into the town and came home, where the tired grandmother in the meantime had rocked the child to sleep.

Already sensual and sentimental, the infant boy had learned that by weeping he could obtain the extra gratification of being sung to and carried in someone's caressing arms up and down, up and down. So he would not let his eyes close when left alone. They had tried to discipline him, but he would stand up in the cot, shaking with willfulness, until he fell and struck his head against the railing. Then the obstinate lament would give way to fainter cries of genuine pain, and someone would give in. His mother could now rarely be the one, and his weight was bound to go on increasing faster than she could recover health. The heat was intense; no one's strength lasted quite all the day.

The brother consulted the younger sister. "The sooner we stop indulging him the better," he said. "A little older, he would bear a grudge for a week, and feel altogether unloved and abandoned and abused. I was like that; even God neglected me. Now he won't mind by morning. Babies haven't much memory."

"We all have to give up luxuries in hard times," the girl said. "Why shouldn't he?"

So they devised a harness of an old pair of suspenders and some strong tape, stitched and knotted, which both the mothers approved. In it he might exhaust his indignation and his self-pity without any risk, free to turn from side to side, but unable to stand up and fall. "From now on," the bachelor said, "no more real injuries toward fraudulent ends." They all smiled deliberately, their mother with a tear. The child's mother, full of her secret shame, said little. She was able to go down to supper the night the experiment was tried.

It was a simple but fine meal of ham and cottage cheese and jelly and milk. Their father, still young in body but anxious about his health, commented upon each dish. The son-in-law, after long hours of vain business, hungry out of proportions to any such repast, hid his disappointment.

The younger daughter came late to the table, having fastened the baby in his bed.

"Is the boy asleep so soon?" the son-in-law asked.

"Oh, not yet."

The son explained as lightly as he could. "We decided he would have to be broken of being rocked to sleep. So we made a harness. He can't stand up and can't hurt himself."

Upstairs he began to cry.

The elder mother said, "It is better that he should be trained now. The older he gets, the harder on him it will be. And on the rest of us."

The son said, "He only cries because he knows that by so doing he can get what he wants. Babies' lives are experimental; they repeat whatever has resulted in pleasure."

The aging man at the head of the table scowled at this pretentious reasoning.

The young girl said, "He is getting heavier every minute. Sister can scarcely lift him now. It is hard for anyone, just at this time of day, when you're tired to death. If he insists on his lullaby very much longer, one of those Polock giantesses up the street will have to be sent for." She tried to make it seem humorous, but her eyes sought her brother's—they had made a grave mistake.

For the son-in-law was not listening to the arguments. He was swallowing his food without chewing it, deaf with resentment, deaf to all but the little cries resounding through the house. It was his child, not theirs. Insolent with a sense of his dependence on them, and without hesitation they were robbing him of his natural authority; were making decisions and educating and punishing his son as they saw fit. And his son was to be a gentleman; why should he be initiated into their sad cult of self-denial? He stared at his wife as if he saw in her only a member of that family.

They all sat in silence while the babe wept.

It was a warm evening almost as bright as noon. This was the weather of the poor; the atmosphere was a sufficient clothing and shelter, and it seemed nourishing—did one actually need much else?

The tired grandmother, less impressed by the baby's crying than by the red face of her daughter's husband, the reactionary expression of her own, made a move to go. "Please don't, dear," her daughter said. "We should just have to begin again tomorrow."

Everywhere else it was the hour of pleasure. And a thousand automobiles were being transformed into vehicles of emotion, illusion; and through the groves young people were going down to the soft-shored lakes to play among the reeds; and in backyards the green clumps of lilac were filling up with fluffy pullets; at that time love usually ceased to torment and turned fecund; and so on. By thinking of these things, the son, unused to home, tried to escape in imagination from the too close reunion.

The lament of the child, losing hope, grew strident. Suddenly the son-in-law dropped his fork on his plate, sprang to his feet, strode over to the window, stepping on his napkin, saying between his teeth, "I will not have a child of mine tied up like that. All your clever theories—what do I care?"

"It can't be helped, sweetheart. Please don't mind. He'll go to sleep in a minute. Please—" his wife pled sweetly, almost without inflection. His brother thought he heard a complaint wilder than the child's, just subdued by that deliberate flat seraphic tone.

"He is too little to be punished," the young father said. He sat down but did not eat.

"Refusing to satisfy him and punishing him are not at all the same thing."

Now his weeping was a low, rasping, almost religious refrain, and seemed to come from a distance.

"I can't help it. I can't stand to hear him howling. I won't. I'm going to clear out if it doesn't stop right away, I tell you."

So powerless against him, it was a simple matter for her to answer firmly. "Very well, dear. Go. You'd better go for a while. I'll telephone you as soon as our child has been disciplined. Run along."

Oh that voice like a deadened bell! Of course the young husband did not move. It was the first time this pair of lovers had had to quarrel with others present; and after birth and death, that is probably the most pitiful moment in existence.

All the eyes around the table had a listless fixity. They all felt their humanity keenly.

So, each one eating without appetite for the others to see, the meal drew to a close. The younger daughter, the maiden despising marriage and comforted by her provisory freedom, did better than the others. But the silence affected her more deeply than the words. She looked at her father because it was he that she loved best. Her brother's eyes followed hers, and this is what they both saw in their father's face: he too was piteously angry.

Though quite out of sympathy with his son-in-law, he had caught his fever of male resentment. He, too, always wanted terribly to be the lord of his home. And now he wanted to be the hero of the scene, envied the scornful sympathy the other inspired and, thinking more and more inaccurately, resented the disapprobation the other deserved. "It ought to be against the law to treat a child like that," he said. "I swear, I believe a woman could be put in jail for it."

The unfortunate young mother could not stand that. Her eyes ran and her cheeks whitened. "Father—" she cried.

Nor could the elder mother endure any more. Long since she had learned never to deny the man she so happily loved, but her heart was not old. She looked shamefacedly at her children. She stood up. "I will not go in. I will just look in. To be sure that he is all right." She fled.

Then the visiting son lost his temper. All his life he had been calculating and, though malicious, mild up to a point—when suddenly, two or three times a year, he would be possessed. Suddenly emotion would break forth, with a sort of harmful brilliance. Then his self-possession was good for nothing but to hurt someone. He could not think and could not say what he thought. All was inspiration and he merely heard himself speak. This began to happen now, with a warning jerking in some nerve or muscle at the back of his head.

The young husband said to his wife, "Your father is right. Your baby is still crying up there. Listen to him. It sounds like a tied-up dog. You don't care what he suffers so long as your relatives say it's all right."

With her napkin she wiped her tears.

The other young man, feeling the worst answers all ready but unchosen, tingling on the tip of his tongue, ran to the door like one taken sick. He could not be sure what the words on his lips were or what they would lead to; he had to reach the door before they could be heard. On the way he stammered aloud, "It does not matter what is the best thing to do, your wife is my sister, your wife is too ill, if the child must be put to sleep, someone else will have to take charge—"

He stood on the porch alone. No one could have understood all that he had said, nor guessed all he meant—what a blessing! His judgment of his brother-in-law (just and pitiful enough in theory, though accompanied by questionable feeling) in any such torrent of instinctively chosen words, would have had no result but to make more nightmarish everyone's distress. Only getting out of doors in time could have checked it; and along with it a parallel plaint, less detailed, less reasonable, in defiance of his father. It was not clear in his mind now. What was most clear was that his own childhood had somehow come back to him, in him. His heart was beating like a child's.

His feeling had not been in logical order and was not yet; some mystery of mistaken identities, or crossed strands of time, lay at the bottom of it. Several persons had figured in the scene as one and the same; he himself had experienced as more than one. He was the grown son and brother, but he had felt like a child. He was also, being so like the weeping child, its real father—not in reality but in truth. And his sister and his mother were the same woman; then his sister's husband might as well have been his father—no, what nonsense! He passed his hand across his face as if to brush away an optical illusion.

This was the trouble: suddenly he had lost all sense of independent personalities, and recognized only composite categories of souls: all the sensitive, brutal, and tragic men, all women fumbling in the spell of love as best they could, and all the children. It seemed to him that there were no real differences of age, but mere subdivisions of one eternally unfledged soul—in infancy, for other's pleasure, accustomed to pleasure; deprived when others were powerless to provide; forming habits by mistake; all to be paid for in due time, and broken. All of them were evidently too poverty-stricken to act upon intelligence. The impotent abandoned what they coveted; the fertile harmed what they begot.

His father joined him, very angry, but with the new dignity of his age. They had planned to pay a visit together miles away in the country that evening. They walked across the soft-sounding lawn. "If your sister cannot do better than this, she will have to find somewhere else to live. For I won't be made miserable another minute, with your modern principles."

"You and her husband have made yourselves ridiculous, that is all. Under the circumstances he should hold his peace. You know it as well as I do. It is not a matter of principle. Sister is sick. She can scarcely hold her baby, much less walk up and down with him until he has had enough of it and falls asleep. Who is there to do it? Mother is tired."

"Well, I won't hear him crying during meals. I'm going to eat in peace. She is stubborn. She always was, when she was little; it's nothing new. You agree with her, of course, because you are like that yourself. But I won't stand it. I'm going to be master in my own house. I tell you, she will have to go."

"Very well, sir. She shall go then. You took her in because they are poor and have no other place to go. Of course your home is your own. And when you've had enough of charity to your children, you've only to say so."

Oh, indeed the past had come back—all of it in disorder. A moment ago it was with his infant nephew that he had identified himself; now as he spoke he was confusing himself with himself as he had been years before, a small boy. Thus his father had provoked him; then, too, there had been talk of youngsters' deserving to be driven from home, of whether or not a father was master in his own house—the poor great-hearted man! Then, as now, unhesitatingly he had replied, the most logically insulting phrase after phrase. He remembered vividly how he had been: slight and pallid, detestably afraid, fighting back in barking tones like some small animal instinctively inspired. So also the babe in his turn, to his father, a few more years having passed, would speak.

But this time the real desperation of father and son did not wake. Their hearts were not in the quarrel; it was not the same. Somehow in the interval they had exchanged a general pardon. Into affectionate indifference their reproaches trailed away. The son noticed how they placed themselves in the automobile, their shoulders in contact, unshrinking.

The father spoke again. "Well, your sister hasn't anywhere else to go. They haven't a cent of money."

"I'll attend to that."

"But you must not burden yourself with their problems. We'll get along. You have your own way to make."

They drove away out between the farms. Now it was night. There were shooting stars, ever falling but not landing; certainly somewhere a hundred adolescent wishes leaped up vainly to meet each one. On porches and in orchards, at pianos here and there, in dimmed automobiles, in impoverished privacy of all kinds, couples were coming together. They passed a number of them. Without doubt, in hopeful tones as if they had been cures for illnesses, marriages were being discussed by these strangers; and chances of people's dying being speculated upon, as if illness were a betrothal with death; and the futures of children fixed, incidentally. Innumerable as bubbles in a restless flood, family circles were being formed or broken—a sighing embrace, a breaking pain. The sounds in the night did not seem appropriate to these grave though common events—only music would have been. Hoarse and faint were the cries of air and water; and the soul's all too quavering.

But recalling the scene at the supper table, the young man thought that utterances more radically tragic had been made there than those in any book or play. When gentle ambitious poor men and women broke down, when domestic pain and want were thus exposed by mistake—were there not dialogues more desperate, reproaches more courageous and opener avowals, than any ever designed by great lyric intellects to reveal evil heroes, or the condemned to death, or saints in ecstasy? Was not existence then stripped more nearly naked? No writer could put these humbler griefs in print. They might in great part be spoken without words; so indeed, an hour ago, they had been. They might take the form of a gaze, or of twisted muscles around one mouth or another, or of a change of color—the rainbow whiteness of dead flesh on some living face. A sentence of death might thus be passed—without any blame theoretically, without even intending to hurt—upon a lover, for example, by his beloved: the expression growing in one second old or (worse still) common, and over the eyes which told the truth, the eyelids kindly sinking shut. Or if a few phrases were spoken, they were too conventional, too discourteous, to have the least poetry. Or they were so obscure, depending for their fatal sense upon so remote and complex an entanglement of incidents, of habits of the heart, echoing so many previous faint phrases, that the whole of a book or play, leading up to them, would not suffice to make their burden clear. In the text of humanity, such were the passages of genius. Thus only could the worst be said; thus only could the lesson, the sentence entirely and accurately characterizing mankind, the summary truth, be expressed.

Then, considering what had happened as a story, he understood that if one added that it had occurred years before, that the babe was now a man, the grandparents dead, the parents old, the uncle (himself) some sort of worn powerful personage, or perhaps a derelict; or if one merely prophesied that in the remote future such things would take place—none of it would be altered fundamentally.

For time is an unreliable thing, he thought; it does not steadily pass but weaves back and forth. At one manifold moment he had felt himself to be a rebellious babe and its imaginary father, his brother-in-law's as well as his father's son, and himself at he knew not what age. He had become a man, but without learning not to feel like a child, not to relapse backward into immaturity for an hour. In a church steeple, alone in the country with its graveyard, past which they drove, he heard ten o'clock strike. So the hour passed; but it would return. Soon he would depart again, to his distant ambitions—the necessary infatuation with himself, the frail glamour of the inappropriate rewards, the remorse incessantly attendant upon his faults—all interrupted here, now, by the experience of his early youth, and all to be interrupted at intervals, always, wherever he was, even by what had happened that day. Always, in an ephemeral western town in himself, in his mind, under a humble roof and as it were amid disunited frustrated elders, there would be the babe weeping, ungratified, bound in its bed, for its own good. The present summer would never quite go by. Time could not be depended upon to sweep him safely, normally, onward; but would be forever letting him fall back into what was over and done with, and letting him, enfevered by the unwanted past, leap weakly ahead into what was to come, to no avail.

And he thought that he (and all other vain men wishing to be strong, even if they could not be strong) might as well resolve to agree with this busy force which no name suited better than another—time or nature or destiny or god or anonym. Maniacal worker, mad about its art, invisible and uninvited, it went on darkening with wild strokes their lives that were but scattered square inches of its design.

Mindreading gambler, it kept playing with them and with facts for unknown stakes. Stern economist, it had meant this part of the West to be poor; and the oppressive forests and sterile hills having been mastered, introduced education and extravagance and optimism and credit to keep living conditions hard as they had been. Just now, as if it had gazed at him personally with its amorous eyes, it had made use of cruel circumstances—poverty and illness and half-incestuous affections—to give him a son, irrespective of his habits and against his will.

In his mind, as he sat beside his good discouraged father, as they drove some miles away from their troubled home, these exaggerated ideas sounded by turns like a harsh Te Deum and a lullaby and a prayerful plea. Could his sister recover? Was the babe, his theoretical son, in good hands, sufficiently strong and not too blundering hands? Mind your own business, he said to himself; God will provide.

The old moon rose; and by its light along the road, he saw, as he had never seen it before, the glacier-built West, electrical in atmosphere, hard at heart: the hills without any consoling vineyards, without placid groups of sheep, and the weedy fields of ripening foods. Whatever had made him think, with vulgar images, when he first returned, that this was an abundant land? It was wondrously poor. Heaven itself might have formed it to be its opposite, a place in which to think of it with desperate longing, with virile love. In the weak moonlight the earth and the air had an appearance of painted clapboards and shaky turrets: dwellings for souls that were untamed and immature. He understood that in spite of changes it was a mystery still, a wilderness, vain and ashamed, waiting its turn to be a good place. And in it, with his dubious abilities and yet rudimentary desires, the baby that he loved, by this time, was asleep.

A Visit to Priapus

Occasionally last winter Allen Porter would mention a young man of sonorous name and address, Mr. Jaris Hawthorn of Clamariscassett, Maine, who as a lover had briefly amused but not satisfied him at all, and who thereafter bored him as a friend. He said that he would not think of introducing him to any of us because (a) he is a bad painter and a pseudo-intellectual, and so obtuse and pushing and clinging as to make any merely social relationship with him a nuisance; and (b) his sex is so monstrously large that sexual intercourse with him is practically impossible. I must say that neither the report of his monstrosity nor of his ambitious and sentimental spirit really dismayed me. For Allen in bed is easily affrighted; and when it comes to talk of art, excesses of friendliness, etc., he has less patience than anyone. With his lively and improper sense of humor, Allen presented this phenomenal fellow to Pavlik, on account of the obscene way Pavlik talks and the freakish pictures he has painted. But nothing came of that, he believed. Pavlik as a rule is unwilling to risk getting caught in such misdemeanor by his darling, Charles, who, I presume, would simply feel authorized by it to go and do likewise or worse.

When Allen heard of my trip to Maine he suggested that I see Hawthorn, *quand même*; we talked some sense and some nonsense about it, and I promised; but evidently he thought me too proud or prudent to do any such thing. Having taken stock of Sorrento and looked at the map, I wrote Hawthorn and proposed our meeting somewhere halfway. He did not reply promptly; and meanwhile Monroe had written that George's keeping company with young Chitwood worried him; so I had begun to worry again, to dream despairingly of Ignazio, and to write those above-mentioned letters. At last an answer came from Hawthorn, matter-of-fact and cordial: he would meet me on the verandah of the Windsor Hotel in Belfast at ten a.m. on Wednesday. I ruefully thought that I was no longer quite in the mood or in the pink of condition for such a meeting; but I did not let myself think much, one way or the other. For it might well turn out to be the sort of folly that I owe it to myself and even others to stoop to upon occasion, according to the rule of my health and my particular morality. And, even if no healthful pleasure was to be had of him at journey's end, no doubt the journey would be of interest. I should see some sea-captains' houses and some variations of the Maine landscape. And it seemed to me that I might turn to stone in Sorrento, to stone or to wood, if I did not go somewhere else, do something.

On Wednesday, Ernest, the bright youth who tends Frances' furnaces, woke me at daybreak; and I gulped some potent warmed-over coffee; and he drove me to Ellsworth where I had to wait an hour for the bus. I was in my most absurd matutinal state, absent and giddy, like one strongly bestirring himself under hypnosis. The bus was of the vast and delectable streamlined type with powerful engine and terrible cry and springs like a dream. At first I thought its motion might make me sick. Maine highways are narrow, with very few motorists on them, but those few are plucky and stubborn. The bus would roar whenever we sighted one, and without slacking up in the least, descend upon him, then suddenly digress and swing around him, with two wheels off the pavement. South of Ellsworth there is a succession of long hills. As we flew down into the valleys between them—so delicately was every bit of shock mollified by the mattress-like suspension under us—we suddenly ceased to feel the road, resuming it with a slight tremor only when we began to climb again. After a certain term of chastity, to say nothing of particular discouragements such as this summer's, I always think of dying, with no very clear distinction between the longing for it and the dread of it. So I was frightened by this ride and somewhat fascinated by my fright. But I forced myself to entertain other thoughts; to admire the poor farms and the old towns through which we passed, and the successive waterways, the play of peculiar Maine light, and the wonderful absence of billboards: a sort of passion and chastity of landscape.

I arrived first at the rendezvous. No reference had been made in my letters or Hawthorn's to my spending the night; suddenly I felt ashamed to be taking all that for granted; therefore I hastily checked my bag inside the hotel. The porch agreed upon was half a block long, separated from the parked cars of Main Street by a jigsaw balustrade; and it had a neat alignment of rocking chairs on it. I sat in a rocking chair and read *Time*. No one else sat; a good many stepped briskly along the sidewalk, and a good many drove in and out of town, on more respectable business than mine, I thought. Then it occurred to me that neither of us had any idea of the other's appearance. I knew only one thing about him, and that one thing, of all I might have known, the least perceptible, the least practicable mark of identification. Which at least brought to my mind the fact that this constituted the worst behavior, the most grotesque episode, of my entire life. What, frankly speaking, was I sitting there waiting for, watching for? It might have been an obscene drawing in the style of El Poitevin or Vivant Denon: a giant phallus out for a ride in a car. And what part would it hold the wheel with, and how would it honk, I asked myself—ribald laughter all provoked but hushed in me, along with other more and more mixed emotion.

Naturally, bitter regret for my great days as a lover assailed me. Also a fresh and terrible kind of sense of devotion to the two whom I love, who love me, who cannot keep me happy, whom I torment and disappoint year in and year out, ached in my grotesque heart. With which my pride also started up, at its worst. To think that I should have come to this: sex-starved, in a cheap provincial hotel humbly waiting for a total stranger; and it should be so soon, at thirty-eight! But, I must say, then a certain good nature quickened in me as well, thank God; an amused appreciation of myself. Once more I summoned up courage to believe—scowling a little, grinning a little, gritting my teeth—that in the considerable brotherhood of middle-aged men in unlucky sexual plight, not many are my peers in this respect and that respect at least. G.D. on the Bowery. A.E.A. or B.K. in Turkish baths: my ventures no doubt are as undignified as theirs, my sensations probably less rapturous than theirs, but . . . But my life is the oddest. As a result of years of perfect intercourse, unforgettable, my self-consciousness is extraordinary. Living as I do, undivorced—with those I have most desired still the closest to me—I am embarrassed in the pursuit of pleasure by their alluring noble example; handicapped by trickery of my own spirit, my own flesh; impoverished by tribute. Nevertheless I have been able to keep a more level and subtle head than G.D., a more fearless temper than A.E.A., a soberer habit than B.K. In the very efficacy of my excitements there is something like a practical morality. My very sense of humor about it all seems somehow poetical. And if I ever have occasion to tell this tale, for example, I shall tell it well. So I said to myself, boasted to myself . . .

By that time, with mechanical eye, I had read *Time* from cover to cover. In any case I could not take any further interest in the sad international facts it so blithely reported, nor any other particular facts, not even the facts of my presence where I was, and why, and what would come of it. I was under an introspective spell. I was interested in only the wondrous tiresome way my mind works, always the same way, no matter what it has to do, incorruptible by what it has to deal with. It was fascination of only the sense of life in general, in the abstract, all of a piece: life of which, like everyone else alive, I am daily, gradually, dying . . . Which mystic fit, as it might be called—in almost entire forgetfulness of time and place and purpose and self—seemed the purest kind of experience of all. It can occur only when one's sense of reality has failed; when one's habitual way of thinking of one's self has broken down somehow. It occurs in sexual intercourse, but, alas, not often.

Then a young man drove up and parked his car, and I recognized him as my Hawthorn. With a sign of relief I noted that he was good-looking, respectable looking. He gazed at me but did not speak. I gazed at him. He turned away toward the main entrance of the hotel; so I waited a few seconds, from second to second, quiet as a mouse, while he went in and came out; and just as I was about to signal to him, he stepped into his car and drove away. That is to say, it was not he. And so it seemed to me that nothing in the world, no beauty, no monstrosity, could possibly stir me out of my absent-mindedness, sense of mysticism, and humiliation. For, said I to myself, I have lived too well; I have loved too truly, which now is all over; and I have thought too much, even in this half hour of Hawthorn's tardiness.

Then there Hawthorn was, in a more expensive car than the wrong young man's. There he was, and naturally he recognized me at once: I had forgotten that I am somewhat a celebrity. And he smiled at me and waved to me. I stepped down from the verandah to the curb, and we greeted each other as if we had been acquainted for years. I got in beside him. We drove a little way, then I remembered my valise, and we went after it. The back of his car was full of oil

paintings for me to "criticize": first indication of one of the peculiarities of which Allen had warned me. For a while naturally I
wanted to forget about the other peculiarity.

First we went to visit the Marine Museum of Searsport, where I
especially admired a ship's model all carved of the pith of the fig tree.
That is the deadest-white substance on earth, whiter than marble,
whiter than lard; but there is a slight parallel grain in it, a faintly
yellow or flesh-colored thread, which shows in the sails, like fairy
stitching. In its present homemade showcase it is drying and
breaking; a bit of weather gets in; and gradually the tiny alternate
storms of humidity and aridity undo the rigging; the tiny companion-
ways all droop. The good gossipy Searsporter who acts as curator
said that it could not be mended.

There are also fine antique chests of rosy wood trimmed with
sallow brass, all smoothed by more or less intentional caresses of
salty chapped hands of sailors dead and gone. There are also a few
Oriental "antiques," including an astrological compass: a saucer of
golden lacquer with a thousand minute scribbles on it—a gift to
newlyweds, to determine the placement of their new house, the
curator informed us. The handsomest object of all was a great pin or
plug intended to be thrust into a hole in the gunwale of a whaler and
entwined with some tackle: a thing of whittled whalebone, of a
lovely flecked color, about the size of a policeman's club or a unicorn's
horn, and indescribably shapely, perfectly tapering, with delicate
flange near the top. Jaris Hawthorn, perhaps a bit proudly hinting
at my real reason for being there with him, laughed at me for my
admiration of it. But I believe that it did not particularly impress me
as phallic; I usually know when I am thus impressed; I have not
much subconscious. Apropos of which, he told me that the men of
the Maine coast often carry little finely whittled wooden phalli
which come in handy as thole-pins, and which they more or less
honestly believe will also cause the lascivious opportunity to occur,

and augment and safeguard their potency once it has occurred. There is a poem by Robert P. Tristram Coffin about this, entitled, "Pocketpiece." Jaris promised to discover and make me a present of one.

Then in the various coast towns, Belfast, Camden, Waldeboro, we devoted some time to what I had spoken of as my objective on this journey: the viewing of old domestic architecture, which must be America's richest heritage of art, and most lamentably unfulfilled tradition. The great residences of shipmaster and lumbermen disappointed me; they show the effect of the intercourse with southern seaports such as Charleston and Savannah, and too much honor has already been done them in the way of servile imitation: post offices, city halls, boarding schools. The small dwellings are the glamorous ones, particularly those of lovely local brick, blocky, with blunt roofs and a minimum of eaves; their austerely cut doors and door-jambs and window-frames set in flush with the ruddy walls, just as in seaman's chests the brass locks and reinforcements are imbedded in the wood.

The modern architect is inclined to bully his client in the name of aesthetics. Let both of them consider this: everyone's evident determination in this part of the world a hundred years ago to have his individual habit and habit of mind and even foible respected and embodied in building. Habit forgotten long since, dead and buried; so what does it matter? It matters in that here in the inanimate lumber, the changeless mineral, there still is emotion, physiognomy, personality. This door-jamb still smiles; that lintel looks haughtily important; this or that stairway has a philosophic or a melancholy or a gratified expression. It is a kind of beauty, and a quality of art, that formal aesthetics can never legislate into being.

One house that I particularly liked is in a precipitous street on a very narrow property. There was no ground on which to erect the horse stable except on a level with the second story; therefore the sympathetic builder ran a wide stairway up to it along the outside of the house, parallel to the sidewalk; and the combined effect, through the cheap and small, is as noble as Perugia. These retired mariners, having seen enough weather on their voyages, evidently dreaded getting wet; therefore most of the barns and woodsheds are under the same roof, continuations from the kitchen, which makes for grandeur as well as the beauty of compactness. Think of what a time I should have persuading modern architects Gropius or Lescage to respect my dislike of open doorways, opaque windows, and my light-shyness to boot, to complicate matters; my dread of overhearing the rest of the family in the next room converse, fidget, sigh.

In this part of Maine the true farmers' barns outside the villages, up on small simple hills, balmy with poor hay, surveying the august and brilliant inlets, are often shingled to the ground like old Long Island houses. In their present shabbiness every shingle catches its bit of light and casts a minute shadow; so they look as if they were bound in sharkskin.

At midday we stopped at an inn of the sort that ladies love, where the classic Maine menu was proudly served us: lobster in milk, hot biscuits, blueberry pie. Somewhat accustomed enough to my companion by that time, I improperly glanced at the antique four-poster beds spread with old hand-stitched coverlets but fitted, no doubt, with new "beauty rest" mattresses. However, for us two, I felt, there would have been incongruity in that rich and dainty interior. Then with polite hypocrisy I told him a story that I had made up to explain my not returning to Sorrento that evening. With no hypocrisy at all he replied that he desired to spend the night with me. But it was his father's car that he was driving, and he had promised to be back with it before dinner. If I accompanied him as far as Clamariscassett it would make my return-trip on the bus only a little longer, that was all. So it was decided.

Next he sat me down cross-legged in the grass where the car was parked, and masterfully showed me all the oil paintings he had brought along to show me. And he had an air of profound respect for my opinion, but of difficulty in understanding it, or of determination not to understand it unfavorably. Usual provincial American landscapes; watercolor conceptions executed in oil, and, alas, effortlessly executed, with a pretty bit here and a strange bit there, probably by accident . . . I kept thinking of Allen—how he must have hated this—with a certain soft hilarity.

Then Hawthorn and I strolled through a shabby meadow and an idyllic little grove, and lay there on the grass, ten or fifteen feet above sea level. The tide was out, leaving a few pools which winked and rippled, and rocks from which the seaweed hung in yellow braids and tangles, and a confetti of shells. The breeze brought up odors of ocean, an odor as herby as pubic hair, an odor as tepid and sweet as saliva . . . At last I felt at ease enough to stop talking. My Hawthorn lay, less at ease, fairly near me, with a mildly joyous grin now and then, and an occasional caress, not unmanly, not really indecent. His little eyes sparkled with perhaps one idea only, but we talked of this and that. Now it was he who was making me talk, questioning, teasing, which at any rate I preferred to my usual nervous, conscientious improvisation.

He was not beautiful. Yet there was nothing exactly unbeautiful about him except his teeth: they were not quite white, and there was one missing, on the right side of his grin. The line of his lips was indented in exact correspondence to the shape of his nostrils. His hair was coarsely wavy, and when the sun struck it, almost as yellow as the seaweed. I liked his hands which, oddly enough, were less ruddy than his face; good fleshy tapering fingers which were not hot, not cold, and not damp. Perhaps I did not like his eyes, in spite of their excitability. It is in hands and eyes that I particularly expect to observe what is called "sex appeal"; that is to say, whenever they have failed to appeal to me and I have gone ahead anyway, I have had a sudden embarrassing disinclination to cope with myself at some point, or a particularly severe disenchantment at last. So I kept looking at these hands and eyes, questioning, whether to go ahead now or to stop.

One learns by experience that it is fatal to ask one's self that specific question too soon; and the right moment is infinitesimal; and therefore as a rule one asks it too late. Furthermore, except by the imaginary process of falling in love, how can one tell, how can one even prophesy, whether or not one will enjoy the body of another— until one has undressed it, touched it, tasted it? And apparently I am never to fall in love again, because I have not fallen out of the loves of my early manhood. Also I am the sort of person with whom no one is much inclined to go to bed without having been induced somehow to fall in love somewhat; which makes it all difficult for me, at least necessitates a certain hypocrisy . . . Now it was too late to try to be sincere. Before I left Sorrento, before I left New York, I had resolved not to stop; it was a matter of principle and a point of honor.

Now and then I withdrew a little distance on the flowery grass in order to take another good look at my man. As his trousers of Palm-Beach cloth were cut, the peculiarity of his physique which so impressed Allen did not appear, and with reference to that I quoted to myself the famous first line of Sterne's *Sentimental Journey*: "They order, said I, these things better in France"; which amused me. All this, I also thought, was rather reminiscent of Sorrento, Italy, than of Sorrento, Maine; which was pleasant. And the very way my mind worked, immoral or mock-immoral, forever similizing and citing and showing off to itself, pleased me. Hawthorn of course had no notion what my several smiles meant, but replied to each with his little energetic self-conscious grin. I enjoyed lying there, comfortably fatigued and careless; perfectly willing but not at all anxious, not eager. For this I had come half way across the state at the crack of dawn. What an odd mood; and it amounted to an odd attitude to take toward a young man reputed to be phenomenal: the oddest by-product of my wearisome dangerous passions all summer long . . .

Now Hawthorn had taken off his Palm-Beach coat and neatly folded it, lest this and that in the pockets disappear in the grass. He wore a loose shirt of silky finished fabric, very dressy in a provincial way. Very tight and bright-colored braces held up his roomy trousers. He lay propped on one elbow, vigilantly watching me, asking rather pointless questions, and giving bits of uninteresting information. I lay flat on my back with one arm up to keep the sun out of my eyes. I pulled blades of grass and chewed the juicy ends, and I teased my own nostrils with the stems of clover which had the plumpest, spiciest heads.

There was magic in the scene, but it was a humorous rather than a poetical or passionate magic. It reminded me of a chromolithograph that I used to have hanging over my desk in Paris; a scene of court-ship about 1900, a young man and woman in boating attire on a river bank under a willow tree. He was in his shirt sleeves with bright braces, his hair parted in the middle, his eye lashes wonderful, his mustaches silkily drooping; and she lay flat on her back under a parasol; and he crouched facing her, no doubt with tremors of the mustaches and wonderful winks—to all intents and purposes my father and my mother, I used to think: a kind of epitomization of the mood in which in 1900 I must have been conceived. Monroe did not admire that chromolithograph, and left it behind in the Rue de Conde when he packed up our belongings . . . But the 1900 young man's eyes were dreamy, idle, cloudy, like a stallion's. Whereas my present young man's just slightly glittered now and then, with a look in the intervals between. Perhaps he as well as I was taking it for granted what deeds of darkness we should do when darkness fell. Yet those glitters were not what I should call sensual glances. His appetite, I gathered, was taking the form of a more and more intense friendliness and admiration. Well, I thought, that would suffice; or perhaps, as Allen had warned me, more than suffice. My appetite, it seemed, was not taking any form at all.

Meanwhile the cool noon sunlight came down the shore at an angle like that of the soft riptide; and hung like spray in the treetops; and rippled on a level with my head through the coarse bloom of the meadow. Down below in the returning water gulls worked or played, conversing a great deal. Their conversation here on the Penobscott, I fancied, was not the same as in Frenchman's Bay. Up there you might have thought them all in poor health or past their prime, retired from the strenuous and profitable business of the open ocean. They spoke tremulously, and with what was like effortlessly controlled temper, in the way of old ladies in a sanitarium complaining of what diet the nurses have brought them on trays . . . I told Hawthorn this; and he beamed, he always beamed, as if every utterance of mine were in perfect rhymed couplets. Also, I thought, there was something amorous about those Sorrento gulls, indecently gossiping, undignifiedly bewailing, like aging homosexuals at a cocktail party, comparing notes; but of course I did not mention this to Hawthorn. Instead I described to him the grief-stricken and perhaps crazy gull on the rock under my bedroom window, and I did so maliciously, to make sure of what I suspected: that it did not interest him; he knew nothing of grief, of true love.

Then some summer ladies wandered from the inn down through the grove with sudden piping voices, which made him blush and draw away from me. This gave me a welcome insight into his state of mind. For there had been nothing overtly improper in the relative positions of our recumbent persons there in the redolent and tickling grass where presently the ladies also would lie and gossip and giggle; but evidently his thoughts were amorous, his conscience bad. I took his embarrassment as a good excuse to bestir myself and get him started toward Clamariscassett. For this self-conscious and inactive felicity of mine would soon wear itself out, if it had not already done so.

When we reached Clamariscassett he introduced me to his family, friendly but not cheerful folk, evidently of modest fortune, somewhat shiftless. Then he asked me to criticize half a dozen more paintings. While I was thus occupied, thus embarrassed, the family terrier bit my ankle, but it did not hurt. Jaris, with money solicited from rich neighbors and vacationers, had built a little information bureau on the main street, which he and his sister administered; and I had to admire this next. The moral support and occasional friendliness of Maine celebrities such as Messieurs Colcord and Coffin, Madams Carrol and Chase, have been useful and gratifying to him, he explained; and now he is planning a small public park in a vacant lot on the waterfront; and we also inspected this lot. Then he marched me a good way up the Clamariscassett River to view its mysterious vast banks of oyster shells: residue of century-long banquets of a prehistoric people. All this tired me: I felt less and less equal to the opportunity that the night was to afford.

Jaris suggested that we sleep at his parents, although his mother would disapprove—the discomfort, not the immorality, he hastily explained; for we should have to share a single bed. I intensely agreed with her. His father needed the car early in the morning, but he offered to drive us to an inn at Pemaquid Point and to fetch us back next day at noon. Evidently it did not occur to these good people that I could be expected to spend the night at the inn alone, which complacence puzzled and amused me.

It was a new building, most absurdly planned and unattractively furnished. There were two double beds in the room over the kitchen assigned to us. The proprietress complained about this fact a little; she had hoped to rent it to two couples; the morals, that is the *moeurs,* of Americans, how odd! To reach the bathroom we had to go downstairs into the kitchen, and through the sitting-rooms, and back upstairs from the front hall. While I went on that expedition, then while I unpacked—as indeed all the day whenever I turned my back a moment—Jaris engaged a cook or a maid or another guest in the warmest conversation. This great sociability, I thought, must underlie his several semi-philanthropies, raising of funds, giving of information, etc.; and went well with other traits of his odd character: a sort of vacuity, and a sort of insincerity. It was evident also that he had confidence in his ability to obscure the issue of his homosexuality. A tireless indiscriminate friendliness no doubt is one good way; for these natives of Maine appear to be not fussily moral, but passionately neighborly, touchily democratic . . .

Then in my black waxed silk, exotic rather than erotic attire, I lay down on one of the double beds and waited for him. From the remote bathroom, and I know not what further conversation on the way there and back, he came at last and lay beside me. Still I could not think whether to like or dislike his eyes, so light-colored, so old-looking, and decidedly aslant, enclosed in numerous little intense wrinkles pointing out and pointing up. Suddenly I knew what I thought: they were half-animal eyes, metamorphosed eyes; the deadness in them was the legendary pathos of the satyr. His strong, thin, and slightly chapped mouth also pointed up. Most modern men smile downward; he smiled in Etruscan style. We gossiped some more; then he took me in his arms.

After a good many vigorous hugs and rough kisses, I observed that he was worrying about my response to them, that is, my lack of response. What was he doing that displeased me, or was it that I lacked temperament, or what? In fact the day had affected me as if it had been interminable, and I was waiting to forget my fatigue. Also our dinner had been of the grossest meat and potatoes and pie, and I was still aware of my digestion. Of course I was embarrassed to speak of these unromantic impediments. Instead I remarked that his Palm-Beach-cloth suit was uncomfortable, scratchy. He promptly removed it.

His hair was only warmly, rustily blond; but his flesh had the rather weak and precious texture, the hothouse pallor, that as a rule goes with red hair. This, in contrast with his sunburned face, made him appear very naked with his clothes off. The muscles of his back were admirable; the backbone in a deep indentation from the nape of his neck to his compact buttocks. He carried himself with a slight stoop, but his chest was round and stout enough to make up for it. The form and carriage of a young day-laborer . . . Having undressed in the opposite corner of the room with his back to me, briskly, methodically, he turned around and faced me with the strangest expression—somewhat joyously exhibiting himself, yet somewhat ashamed, and perhaps resentful of my interest, my amusement—and came to bed; and the seemingly interminable night's work or play began.

His sexual organ, the symbol of this silly pilgrimage, and also the cause of my severe self-consciousness and unromantic sense of humor, really was a fantastic object. No matter what infantile prejudice you might be swayed by, or pagan superstition, or pornographic habit of mind, you could not call it beautiful; it was just a desperate thickness, a useless length of vague awkward muscle. An unusual amount of foreskin covered it, protruded from the end of it, thickly pursed like a rose. In the other dimension also, around the somewhat flattened shaft, the skin was very coarse and copious. Neither in length nor breadth did it increase in the usual ratio, nor did it grow quite rigid, at least not until it had almost reached the point of its difficult orgasm. And at that point, as I presently found to my discomfiture, it was apt to fail suddenly, droop suddenly, lie useless half way down his thigh. But still in dull and futile flexibility it had a look of pompous, ominous erection. It was a thing which to a happy person of normal spirit would be a matter of indifference, an absurdity; which on the other hand, to a very sensual man or woman who happened to have a faulty understanding of his way of life, might be a cause of, or a pretext for, desperate bad habit and disappointment. And now here was I, certainly unhappy, and dangerously sensual, but no fool, and not afraid—here was I in bed with Priapus! A thing to frighten maidens with, and to frighten pillagers out of an orchard; a thing to be wreathed with roses, then forgotten . . .

The mind of poor Priapus in bed seemed to me no less exceptional and troubling than this classic bludgeon. You might have expected him to take pride in it as a kind of wonder of nature; or you might have expected him to hate or pity himself on account of it, or to have a horror of being desired for that and no other reason— expectations far too simple. Upon my referring to it he only conventionally and complacently demurred, as if that were a customary flattery, due tribute, and entirely agreeable. But when I paid attention to it more directly than by word of mouth, active attention, then its size and strength would suddenly decline: the flesh itself ashamed. You might think that such a thing, in its hour of exercise, must cast some spell upon the one of whom it is so disproportionate a part, upon his entire temperament, even his opinion and his emotion. It was not so. Never for an instant did my Hawthorn cease to be self-possessed, critical, and equivocally self-critical, and with the oddest air of begrudging, of calculatory cunning. A man of the purely mental type, pretending to be erotic . . . It absurdly occurred to me that he might be a man quite deficient physically to whom some wondrous physician, or compassionately interfering friend, or capricious deity, had simply attached this living, but rather spasmodically living, dildo.

And what a strange type: a mentality as busy as a bee, and forever blushing or turning pale; feeling devilish or feeling pure; and in an instant beginning to be sad or angry, but the next instant overcome by fond satisfaction, and self-satisfaction! All night long, throughout my own easy enjoyment and my laborious effort to please him, my falling asleep irresistibly and his waking me, and the rise and fall of that practically hopeless phallus, all night long he was evidently thinking, thinking, in that inconsistent way of his. Thinking, thinking: explaining himself a little, at least to himself; justifying himself a little, or trying to decide how to go about justifying himself if he should have to; and resenting little things I did or things I said, but losing track of his resentment at once, all absorbed in some sort of theory of love, or policy of being my lover, or dubious general scheme of loveableness. While the light bulb without a shade over the bed was on, I could not help seeing all this, kaleidoscopic in his face: all this disorderly rationalization, moralizing, this cold and interminable changing of his mind. I tried not to care; I looked away from his face, and my naturally erotic eyes were indeed otherwise fabulously occupied. I shut them; I turned off the light. But in the dark I could feel the same incongruity in the various emphasis of his fingertips, straining of his thighs, stiffening of his neck—an intellectual straining and stiffening.

I said to myself that he must so admire intellect that he encouraged himself to think as much as possible, no matter what; it was like being in bed with a kind of German philosopher. And probably his intelligence has never quite sufficed to put in order and clarify even for himself the incessant ejaculation of these pseudo-ideas. Certainly his speech never sufficed for an instant to convey to me anything that I could be quite sure of, or entirely respect. Every now and then he whispered something, but never a whole sentence: a word or two, then a silence, then a soft stammer, with a shrug, with a little grimace. Every now and then whatever I did obviously shocked him. But he was ashamed of himself for being shocked. So then almost instantly he would make up for it by an added word or two in explicit praise of my unembarrassed eroticism. Twice in the night he said that he hoped to be influenced by me and become like me in that respect. Evidently he assumed that this intimacy of ours, so rashly and improperly improvised—what for?—was to go on indefinitely like a marriage made in heaven . . .

Naturally at times I grew as inappropriately thoughtful as he. I simply wearied of lying in the dark, vainly clasping insensitive pseudo-Priapus; I despaired of ever understanding that petty morality, or ever discovering just what would undo and overcome that giant concupiscence. Therefore I would turn on the light again, and by some calculated caress keep him from speaking. Then I would see a sort of apathy, an expression of boredom and disinclination, gradually accumulate in his face, tight-mouthed, dead-eyed. Oh, that eye of his, retrospective even upon the present object, like the eye of a sea gull! If he noticed my observation of him, instantly he would respond with his little Etruscan grin, lips up, eyes up; and the impression that made was of entire insincerity, I think he must have sensed it; for he would kiss me with a fiercer approximation of appetite, or give me a special series of rapid and muscular hugs.

It was bound to be difficult, having to do with a physique such as that: a thing rather symbolic of sex in the abstract than apt to do the actual work of intercourse in any way that I know of. At a glance I could guess how long it would take, how lethargically, callously, it would function: which did not dismay me. What dismayed me little by little was to learn that it was very sensitive as well, more troubled than troublesome—like the sex of some shy wild animal, in incalculable kind of rut one minute, and a strange state of arbitrary chastity the next minute; or like the sex of a great will-o-the-wisp, shrinking away in the darkness. The abnormality, the practical or mechanical trouble, was bad enough; but it was the inability to concentrate, the subnormality of emotional temperature, which made it impossible. No matter, I said to myself; no doubt love or even lust would find a way in time; practice makes perfect . . .

But a certain uncomfortableness of spirit, obscurity of point of view, is likely to keep one from falling in love, and virtually discourage even the lesser or lower forms of desirous imagining; the spirit is prevented from going to work with any ardor to solve the problems of the body. In the case of male in love with male, this is serious, because homosexuality is somewhat a psychic anomaly, not exactly equipped with mechanism of flesh. At least at the start of such a relationship one must fumble and feel one's way amid a dozen improvised, approximative, substitutive practices. From start to finish many men find this a terrible disadvantage, a continuous punishment: the worry of what to do and what not to do, and why not and what next and what else; and the dread of the other's modesty or immodesty or other inexpressible sentiment; and the chill of sense of responsibility, the grievous anxiety of perhaps failing to do for the other what he needs to have done, even amid the fever and rejoicing of one's own success, at the last minute. In bed with such a fellow as my poor Priapus you would have to be phenomenally unkind or perverse not to suffer from this.

That fantastic plaything might have meant nothing to me at all; it was in fact almost good for nothing; it would have seemed only a fearful, comical, mythological, theoretical thing—unless I had been able to command myself to care about it extremely, unless I had deliberately yielded to a kind of drunkenness of caring: wild exercise of the sense of touch, and spurring on of every other nerve from head to foot around it, and intentional blindness to all else, and conscious fetishism, and so on. I may say that I was quite successful in the management of myself in this respect. With a great store of sexual energy saved up in melancholy and inaction, I did care; I was drunken. But the more successful my excitement, naturally the more difficult it was to control myself, to bide my time, to keep from spending. I could continue with enthusiasm and without crisis for one hour, let us say, not for two; or perhaps for two hours, but not three. And whenever I made any special impatient effort to bring him to the point of felicity, or to keep my own pleasure going, or to distract my attention lest it go too far, then I would encounter suddenly the embarrassment of his mind, the defeatism of his flesh; then I would have to begin all over again. All night long in this way it was a little like nightmare: fighting an infinitude, or running infinitely nowhere. He reminded me of the old man of the sea, Proteus, becoming this and that and the other thing as one wrestled with him. I reminded myself of Tantalus in hell, thirsting to death up to his neck in fresh water, starving to death under a ripe fruit-tree . . . And whenever my mastery of myself foiled, the nightmare ended for the time being, that is to say whenever I succeeded in spending—there he was still, in his stubborn capricious pretentious condition, pretending that he was going to spend presently, and wildly enthusiastic about me, so he said: optimistic as a madman, energetic as a day-laborer.

Thus it went on all night, at least six hours of the night in action, clinging and pressing and striving. I spent three times, which I may say, surprised me. Twice he consented to go to his own bed and let me take a nap; but back he came, apologetic, conceited, coldly sweet. He did not spend until dawn; then so suddenly and softly that I did not notice it. Our room there above the kitchen was large and low: the ceiling drawn down shadowy like a tent to a pair of little windows knee-high. And I was noticing the daylight venturing just then in under those tent-flaps and horizontally across the rumpled beds toward my pillow in the corner. How glad I was to see it! Hours of the next morning sightseeing, hours of the next afternoon in the stream-lined bus on my way back to Sorrento; how restful they would seem, after this peculiar darkness! For another hour or two, only an hour or two, this terrible companion would keep winding upon and around me like a great lively root of a tree, hungry, thirsty; and I felt more and more like a clod, like a stone, but with certain drops of moisture within me still, surprisingly. I noticed only a softening of his shoulders and his thighs, a soft kick such as an infant might give in sudden slumber. Then he whispered to me what it was. It was his orgasm; and it seemed in the nature of a weakness, a lapse, a breakdown; as if at last fatigue made him faint . . .

Evidently it had always been his habit to wield that superhuman phallus against one bent over in his crotch, head downward; so that when finally his moment approaches and he does just as he likes, and it must be in its entire bulk and strength, then precisely one feels it least. I scarcely felt it at all. This was the final instance of the alternation and confusion of too fanciful state of mind and too gross flesh which had characterized this intercourse from the start. Which at that point not only disappointed me; it worried me, in the way of an odd equivalent of bad conscience, a peculiar suspicion of my own honesty and sanity through this experience. The phallus of a demi-god, nightmarish bludgeon, vanishing at last, just as the day began to break . . . It was as if I had made it all up for myself, to please and cheat and defeat myself; and if I had done so in fact, indeed I might well have been ashamed or alarmed.

But what on earth is stranger than the benefit of sexual inter-course to those who feel the need of it? I honestly believe that it is not only politic but moral to comprehend and to admit that strange-ness. For a long time I have had to live in wretched deprivation. Therefore I thanked God—and I mean, I really mean my own pecu-liar, exciting, painful, but certainly trustworthy god or gods—even for an oddity, even for an indecent comedy, like this. Having spent, my Hawthorn at last let me alone. Having slept a while, I began to turn restlessly this way and that in my double bed, so as to get out of line with the early blond rays of the sunrise; I began to hear the ready voices of the maids in the kitchen beneath us brewing weak coffee and frying cheap bacon; I woke up; I got up—feeling like a wild fowl, light and brave.

When I am happy, then I most sincerely wish to comprehend, to detect, to dissect. What man is not worth studying? Surely this young monster of Maine was, especially with strange myself in this curious combination . . . When I am happy, I am also as humble as can be. Therefore I did not conclude that he was simply somewhat impotent, although that fantastic grandeur of his sex might mean almost anything, and not improbably just that. But almost anyone may be impotent with someone. I am not an Adonis; I am the opposite of a Priapus; Maine Priapus simply may not have found me exciting. None of those I have gone to bed with just lately has. Only half a dozen all my life have—and then not really until I had a chance to deploy other aspects of myself than my sketchy, faulty physique; to devote a great amount of time and energy and intellect to their general advantage. I admit this, not complaining of it, but in order to conclude my disgraceful story with due scruple. The disgrace was more than mere physical indifference to me personally this time; there were complications.

In the course of the next morning I questioned him a little about his way of life, his past; and as I interpreted certain of his embarrassed but not in the least unwilling answers, they cleared up much of the mystery. He said that he has not been accustomed to being the beloved, that is, the one desired and labored over; therefore probably my positive active enthusiasm did not suit him. The lovers he has generally enjoyed have been young state-of-Mainers of an exceedingly simple manliness, fisherman and such. It is to be supposed that as a rule such young men never think of intercourse, certainly not of homosexual intercourse, until they are desirous to the point of overflowing. Therefore their excitement may be consummated, overcome, liquidated, in a jiffy. Then no doubt Hawthorn has gone on clinging to them in practically unselfish tribute of enthusiasm, and thrilled by fundamental incompatibility—which in fact affects many homosexuals as oppositeness of sex does not—until at last he has happened to spend, no matter how, as it were a swoon or a sweat or a shedding of tears: a culmination equivalent to exhaustion. Perhaps, truly juvenile, these youngsters have enjoyed his energy and obstination as a kind of nocturnal horseplay or roughhouse. Or perhaps they have only allowed it, endured it. Poor ambitious boys, grateful for the fuss made over them, hopeful of advantage or advancement, often do serve their elders or supposed betters thus: with a kind of venality not quite cynical, not exactly economic. Or, if they have not even allowed it, then poor Hawthorn has had to fulfill the experience for himself at his leisure, in retrospect, in lonely fancy and worshipful dreams and memorial masturbations. And no doubt some new youth has come to his attention whenever retrospect has ceased to operate . . . In any case pleasure must have come to be associated in his mind with failure to have his own way. Desire must seem to him, not what the word ordinarily, exactly intends—the conception of, and strong instinctive urge toward—but an end in itself; felicity itself, whatever the outcome. Which is idealism in a way. And I, my bizarre mystic opinions notwithstanding, am a materialist.

This customary intercourse with facile, normal youngsters also explained that odd trick of tucking his terrible sex away down between his own thighs. A kind of involuntary coition; only impulsive hugging with an orgasm at the end by accident, not planned at all, not noticed much, an overflow, a pollution. At the age when the proletariat is prettiest, that suffices; and when it is a question of only a substitute for normal intercourse, more than that might give offense. Thus I put upon a vague set of unknown, otherwise innocent individuals a slight specific part of the onus of my disappointment . . . It is strange to think how, upon almost every first occasion of love, even every careless fornication, there is jealousy in a humble innocuous form, a token payment of that immense debt to nature—some such grudge against protagonists of the beloved's past; some vague objection to whatever, up to that point, has influenced him, educated him. But one unlucky human being, such as I, may not seriously blame another, such as my Hawthorn, for the gradual effect of the kind of sexual intimacy he has had a chance to engage in. For perhaps one may control the playing of one's own part in love and the like; but the casting of other actors with one is fate: one lives a good deal by accidental meetings.

However, I could not help thinking that in the way of important experience of love—such as my own, in the past, alas—my phenomenal young man's prospects were especially poor. Even in the midst of my enjoyment, it seemed to me: How unlikely that anyone would really wish to keep him for a lover long! Desirable he might appear, indeed, in so far as desire is distinguishable from hope; and in the long run, it is the recollection of delight that constitutes desire. The effect of a hopeless excitement in the end is to weaken one in amorous action; of which in fact I suppose that the sloth of his astonishing flesh is itself an example. Or perhaps the usage of that great fraudulent phallic symbol might just desperately intensify one's desire for someone else, someone less difficult. And I thought it would scarcely be worthwhile to be desired by him, labored over by him. Evidently his pleasures had not even been satisfactory enough, and probably never would be, to instruct him in the giving of pleasure. In any case it would take a long time for me to instruct him in that sense: night after night without a wink of sleep, month after month of exasperation. Thus my widowed, therefore loose imagination tried to peer into the winter months ahead, when he planned to be in New York.

The strangest thing, the worst complication, was that he evidently thought of himself—or at least wished me to think of him—as already seriously attached to me. Every now and then, all night in little truces of his stammering and self-censorship, he made the warmest protestation of his enjoyment of me, his admiration of me, and almost love. I could see almost-love as it were in the balance on his little strong thin lips: the shape of the words without sound. And the slight grimace with which he withheld it or withdrew it implied no uncertainty or insincerity; only a kind of etiquette, a strategical or political sense. Probably he had heard that one should never be the first to say it. No sign of common skepticism, common sense; in every way he seemed perfectly pleased and excited, that is, in every way except that which just then concerned me: the organic, the orgastic. And as I have already mentioned, he murmured optimistic and indeed presumptuous little plans of our continuing to make love regularly and as a matter of course all winter. But why, why, I wondered—since, especially in terms of his eroticism, it all seemed very nearly inefficacious.

Presently an answer occurred to me. It was that vague and no doubt lovely company of young fisherman which suggested it also. The mediocrity of his pleasure did not matter to him because he had an eye on a more important advantage. It was that same not exactly economic venality; that which must have inspired their beguilement of him, their indulgence of his interminable embraces. Indeed our inequality was more complex than that between them and him. In actual amorous effect, mine was the more youthful and potent and expeditious body. But I was the elder in fact; his social and economic superior. No restless boy in his teens was ever more intensely pre-occupied with the future than he, more pathetically determined to get on in the world. And I personified the world: society and celebrity and luxury and, indeed, that worldly opinion which would be favorable or unfavorable to him as a painter.

Yes, I concluded his ardor in my arms, such as it was, had to do with all that, and with my poor physical person only associatively, and by courtesy, and on purpose. He desired me no more or less than a girl-crazy fisherman, a lovely whittler of thole-pins, a snobbish inquisitive parasitic adolescent, might desire him—rather less, probably: for of course he could easily give such a one the immediate satisfaction which I found it almost impossible to give him. Call this a sort of love if you like; surely it was the farthest thing in the world from lust. It was an intellectual effort, a moral embrace. There was indeed not the least indifference about it; but it was only admiration and ambition disguised as desire; in that sense it was fraudulent. It was wily Proteus impersonating Priapus . . . Happening to wear that ostentatious organ, that heavy heraldry of sex, that sacred-looking simulacrum, he more or less consciously would have it serve him as a means to an end, a pretext, an allurement; and as a substitute for what it symbolized, which was what he partially lacked. The entire night was booby-trap; and sex was the bait; and I was the booby. His worst anxiety was lest I perceived this. It evidently meant so much to him that, before I even tried to explain it to myself, instinctively I pretended not to perceive anything. Of course, for my own enjoyment, I needed to fool myself a little also; but only a little, and not all night, and certainly not next morning. During our last whispered conversation before daybreak, I ceased to pretend, in my naturally shameless fashion. His frigidity or difficulty must be my fault somehow, I said. All night long the contact with his body had kept mine in a state of extraordinary tension; therefore the failure or near-failure of our meeting must be due to a lack of physical magic on my part for him; and I said I was sorry. Whereupon he protested that it was not so, not so at all; there had been no frigidity, no difficulty, no failure. And he spoke with an accent of real despair and bad temper.

So I understood that I was not to be allowed to give him up as a bad job and regretfully retreat. He would follow with his peculiar ambitious infatuation, and no doubt self-pity and bitterness. It did not suit him to understand what I might mean by any politely in-sincere word of humility, apology. And at the last, when his orgasm so surprisingly occurred, it was my impression that he felt not only pleasant unusual sensation but a kind of sudden sadness, sorriness. For now, if we continued this intimacy next winter as he intended, there would be this precedent of his being able to have an orgasm at last; I might expect it of him; and I thought he was sorry about that. For he wished to bend and accustom me to the combination of exor-bitance and inadequacy which characterized him physically. It did not suit him to have much of anything expected of him. He wished to compromise me, to engage me in a kind of collusion in the matter of his physical insensibility to me. He wished to feel free to disap-point me, if need be; and to be sincerely surprised by and resentful of my disappointment if I should so far forget myself as to voice any.

I concluded that in a more general sense also he might be a bad-tempered man; at least one of those who must make sure every instant, by hook or crook of their own opinion, of being entirely in the right. I was also reminded of a particular kind of ruthlessness and self-righteousness and spite that had nothing particularly to do with sex: that of many men brought up in hardship or in severe northern places when they arrive to seek their fortune amid those who appear to have been born undeservedly, effortlessly, in a sunny clime or in fortune's lap: New Englanders in New York, Scots in London, Germans everywhere. No doubt I should have trouble with this New Englander if and when I should attempt to cease to be friends with him. But no doubt he would not succeed in having his way with me; for he seemed not nearly pathetic enough to exercise the only intimidation as to which I am weak. Once or twice he frankly referred to his dread of perhaps being disappointed in me in the future. Never for an instant did he show the least interest in, or humility with respect to, the possibility of my having been disappointed by him, then and there, in the present nocturnal circumstances. It may have been only ignorance, innocence; but it vexed me, it warned me. Oh, woe, I exclaimed to myself, woe to whoever happens to be truly fascinated by the sight and the pseudo-promise of that supernatural private part of his! As for me, the characteristic laboriousness of my thought, all one incessant exorcization—to say nothing of my labors upon paper . . . My right hand, with pen in it, enables me not only to learn but to unlearn terrible things, in the long run.

At last we descended from that comical unlucky bedroom, and spent half the morning strolling along the ocean; and sitting on great shelves of vivid granite crosshatched by the millennial waves; and watching two or three families of bathers, none glamorous, on a weedy strong-smelling beach; and chatting of our friends and of modern morality and modern art. It was gloriously sunny; and the little successive scene along shore and across estuary could not have been more beguiling, or more truly American in style: almost every shape in the foreground big and simple; almost everything in the distance little and distinct, speckled and spotted like birds' eggs; the light as specific as the hand of a miniature-painter. My Hawthorn, very proudly native to all this, told me which subjects he had already painted, which he had selected for future endeavor. I spoke encouragingly and suggestively, but it seemed a waste of time. His way of painting is not quite inappropriate for the simple reason that it is amateurish, literal. But with his shaving-brush brush work and muddy stirring together of miscellaneous squirts from inexpensive tubes of paint, how could he approximate all this American surface as of taffeta, this brilliance as of enamel, these clean lively shapes as of a school of fish?

The style of our more accomplished landscape-painters is inappropriate. For example, their preference for backgrounds of blurred air and fused foliage, inspired by the late Venetians, Rubens, Claude: I suppose they will never get anywhere until they cease that. Instead, surely, the right style for our scenery would derive from, or at least be comparable to, the bird's-eye of, let us say, Lucas van Leyden or even Patinir or, indeed, Brueghel: bright-colored as birds' eyes also. I do not think it essential for a painter to have much knowledge of the history of painting; but I soon run out of vocabulary, talking to one who has not.

Then we visited another marine museum, a small collection housed in a handsome old round fortress on Pemaquid Point, marine only in a manner of speaking, inclusive of unsorted bits of bone, stopped clocks, foxed engravings, teacups, and spindles—the ocean through tiny military windows shining in like crystal on fire. Finally the elder Hawthorn came for us; and back in Clamariscassett, we had a hearty meal of crustaceans and berries as usual.

Bit by bit then, Hawthorn told me what resulted from Allen's introduction of him to dear Pavlik: one of the latter's characteristic tyrannical, farcical, talkative little orgies . . . He came to their rendezvous accompanied by none other than, alas, his protégé Ignazio, George's Ignazio, my Ignazio; and then took them both to the flat of one Sylvester Dick, where he urged, or, perhaps, to be exact, ordered them to take all their clothes off. Which Hawthorn did with some unwillingness and misgiving, he told me. But, not having had much variety of sexual experience, he was interested to see what would happen and how it would affect him. And, as a provincial, he felt that in Rome one should do as the Romans do; that is, in New York, he should do as the Russians do. And it pleased him to participate a bit in the private life of so celebrated a painter.

Ignazio's beauty thrilled him, he said; and he assured me that Ignazio also somewhat fancied him. But they exchanged only a few caresses. Pavlik meanwhile not only poured forth his usual improper eloquence, but kept urging them to go ahead and do what they wished to do: which may have weakened their wishing. Also apparently he and Sylvester were all set to join in any amorous action they might commence: a prospect which, for all his admiration and good-sportsmanship, Hawthorn did not relish. Then Pavlik and Ignazio withdrew to a bedroom for twenty minutes. Hawthorn drew the natural conclusion, and was vexed and saddened by it. Upon their reappearance, Pavlik urged, that is, ordered, Hawthorn to stay there with Sylvester; and he and Ignazio departed. Then, upon specific and shameless request, phenomenal phallus was implanted phenomenally in Sylvester's person. My inexperienced provincial was even more surprised that it should be possible than I was to hear of it. He enjoyed it, but soon intensely disliked Sylvester, he said. Whereas he had not forgotten Ignazio's beauty; and Pavlik promised for them to meet again this winter.

To this coarse tale I listened with very mixed emotion, naturally. I replied with somewhat cunning characterization of dear Pavlik, cunning although honest: how he occasionally likes to maneuver his young acquaintances into awkward posture or scandalous relationship, to couple them, and avidly watch their courtship or intercourse, and perhaps slip a little in between them, and playfully uncouple them again—the wind of his strange spirit blowing where it listeth. It gratifies his terrible mental sensuality; or serves to furnish his great draughtsman's imagination; and flatters his sense of his own moral and social superiority. I refer not only to the occasional evenings of amorous fooling, indecent eyewitnessing; his general friendliness toward his inferiors, advising and interfering and gossiping, is in much the same spirit. And, as I warned Hawthorn, he does not as a rule show much respect or esteem for the young men in question, at least not unless they have seemed perfectly obedient.

My warning was perhaps unnecessary. For Hawthorn proceeded to congratulate himself warmly upon being altogether too idealistic and "wholesome" for such goings-on. Also, Pavlik had taken no interest in him as a painter. Perhaps Pavlik would not wish to be friends with him. In any case, he guessed he did not care or dare to be friends with Pavlik. Needless to say, my rather heartsick and half-hearted malice was with reference to his possible future intimacy not with Pavlik, but with Ignazio.

For here I was back where I started, back in the trouble I had left behind in New York: desire for Ignazio and love of George, the first in a way a substitute for the second; and the present grotesque absurd intimacy only as it were a substitute for the substitute. Absurd and perhaps terrible error; anomalous idealism, idealism always mixed up now with immoral realism, and jealous or envious despairing; and the present little fit of jealousy of daft Pavlik and ridiculous Hawthorn with respect to beauteous Ignazio only a parody of my principle passions . . . Fortunately, when I have spent the night in anyone's arms, even coldblooded Hawthorn's, I can regard practically anything with equanimity; practically nothing seems desperate.

Ignazio assured George that he never yielded to Pavlik; and it may be so. The twenty minutes at Sylvester's which made Hawthorn nervous may have been quite inactive. I can imagine my old friend just talking, talking, in his own honor, for his own entertainment; even preaching some, in his unique Manichaean manner; and certainly advising his protégé not to have much to do with Hawthorn, for this or that subtle reason. In fact, his established darling seems to satisfy him sufficiently; in any case he knows how to check him. As he himself once explained to me in a wonderful conversation, he deliberately encourages himself to think and talk as pornographically as possible and not as a preparation for active immorality or jazzy accompaniment, but as a substitute for it. With a mind excessive in everything, overwrought and over-optimistic, if he really did as a number of his close friends do, or if he did all that he himself would like to do, in fact he would lack strength and tranquility for his art. Year in and year out, at any hour of the day or night, especially after dinner, he is likely to get on the subject of sex, his hobby-horse, always with emphasis upon the actual or imagined magnitude of whatever private part comes in question: his very brain, in an extravagant correspondence to its theme, tumescent, erectible. Around and around and around he talks, and, you might say, all up in the air, like a witch astride a broomstick. Those of us who are not simply disgusted by this habit are often much alarmed by it; he might go crazy. But truly, so far, it has been in the nature of a sane wickedness rather than insanity. It is not degradation, but a "sublimation"; not a mania but only idée fixe; not satyriasis, but a kind of cult worship . . . Also he likes to make people think that he fornicates tremendously, with all and sundry, harum-scarum. Many would make fun of him if they supposed that his bawdy was all smoke and no fire, all bark and no bite; he must prefer to seem abhorrent or alarming. Also the general credulity adds zest to his daydream of himself; throws a light of reality upon his purposeful fiction. I am sure that, as to the twenty minutes at Sylvester's, he wanted Hawthorn to think the worst. And, if I were to remind him of that occasion, I should not be surprised to be given to understand that he had enjoyed Hawthorn also, with wondrous abominable details.

I recount all this—not insisting upon the precision of any item, but, I think, generally veracious—as a sidelight upon my old friend's character and, indeed, his art. And the thought of him is helpful to me, enlightening. Indeed I must say that it is an enlightenment in wild disparate flashes, with bad awe-inspiring shadows. For in many respects his sex life has been like the sex lives of those I referred to while shamefully waiting for Hawthorn in the hotel at Belfast—of the kind that gives me an excuse to congratulate myself upon my own ventures, comparatively speaking; the repetitious, lowly, morbid, clownish kind. In other respects it is wonderfully symbolic of the terrible effort I too must make in my way; the policy of high thinking and low behavior to be pursued for art's sake and (in my case, not his), even for love's sake as well. He is a truly remarkable artist. He is certainly demented in a way, and not just figuratively speaking. But he suddenly stops the dancing prancing reeling progress of that dementia, right on the brink of his precipice. There on the brink he cheats it, and casts a beneficent spell upon himself, and turns some of it into art. That is why, when his art appears practically evil, then it is most beautiful, most important.

As for Ignazio, and whether or not he did make or might make love to Pavlik, or to others, even this latest "lover" of mine who told me the above tale: it is a distinction which could not in any case make much difference to me. Even were I to begin caring for him again, hoping to have better luck with him presently in changed circumstances, the report of his mere lolling about and exhibiting himself at Pavlik's behest with that other incongruous couple would discourage me plenty. Hopeless as I am, perhaps I prefer to think the worst, whatever is worst; for George and I have already paid too dearly for our interest in him.

The meal of lobsters and huckleberries and the tale of bawdy ended, it was time to go to a certain drugstore and buy my ticket and wait for the bus back to Amalfi. It was not on schedule, because all morning there had been thunderstorms all up and down the coast.

The drugstore atmosphere troubled me with too many souvenirs of past waiting or loitering, even some pertaining to faraway adolescence: Wisconsin drugstores with Adelaide Bovery or with Roy Kilhart. That is perhaps the most universal and standardized atmosphere in this country. It was hard to believe that outdoors there was Maine's peculiar stormy brilliance, and a block or two away, vast commencement of a series of majestic waterways, and isles as shapely as the Isles of Greece, and an intelligent architecture, and no billboards. Shadowy indoors full of twinkling of bottles and irritating imperative slogans; tableful of magazines glimmering with movie-star faces, platinum-blondes and redheads; odors of syrups and of chemicals; and the sullen chemist in his enclosed corner like a priest in the confessional or a witchdoctor ready to bewitch; and the lazy sweaty boy behind the soda fountain with a cold-sore on the left side of his smile, with platinum-blond hairs on his voluptuous forearm . . . I felt tired of it all, past and present; perhaps of this country; or tired of myself as part and parcel of the tiresome things I was tired of.

We ordered ice cream sodas to pass the time; and I carried mine to a table as far from the fountain as possible, to prevent Hawthorn's conversation with and getting me involved in conversation with the soda-jerker, a friend of his. He nudged me when a certain other young man came in and made a purchase and went out: one whose loveliness a year or two ago had preoccupied him. I could imagine it; but he had lost a number of his teeth; also his complexion bore witness to overindulgence in perhaps ice cream sodas. But now my interest in the not exactly imaginable things Hawthorn had to say about him was a bit forced.

My attention turned back to Hawthorn himself. Whether by night or day, whether on the seashore or in bed or in a restaurant or this drugstore, there was not the least sign of our intimacy's having had an effect on him. He was an inconsequential, that is, a non-sequential fellow, I thought; therefore he was incorrigible. And the incorrigible is practically the eternal. So then and there—in the drug-store, where there was no magic, no charm of scenery or uplifting interest of art or architecture; after lunch, when my desire had expired, and my wish to get away from him was as pronounced as a physical condition—he seemed more important to me than he had seemed before.

Proteus, Priapus: yes, I had thought of those great names, but only descriptively, with no sense of effect upon myself, no awe. Proteus the unknowable, old man of the sea, fish-blooded; personification of indecision and delusion and fraud. Great exciting unpleasant Priapus, embodiment of sex as it may have been set up eternally to intimidate us and to punish us with not pleasurable, no indeed, unendurable club . . . Religious I am, in a way; religious enough to respect and fear such concepts as those two when they come to mind—religious in the sense of a profound persuasion that every-thing must be significant, anything may matter. In which sense I fancied, as it were to pass the time, but with a great grave cold emotion, with a genuflection of all my intellect and every nerve from head to foot—there in the stuffy shadowy drugstore, amid the candy boxes and the patent medicines and the movie magazines—I fancied that those two divinities, oddly two-in-one in the priapic person and protean personality of my odd Hawthorn, perhaps had appeared in my life and come to my mind to show me something or do some-thing to me.

The god of the orchard and the garden perhaps, according to Mediterranean tradition, to remind me to keep what little virginity I have left; to frighten me out of this particular orchard and garden, realm of pornographic imagining and make-believe love and substitute sex; to discourage any further thievery of this kind of exorbitant fruit, this not necessarily unwholesome and not unnatural and in my opinion not immoral but forbidden—somehow, in the long run, by the nature of things, forbidden—fruit . . .

The opposite god, the god of metamorphoses and hopeless strife and vain labor, the opposite of animality and orgy—manifest in all my laborious attempt to understand my little man's odd, infinitely equivocal, perhaps meaningless character, and in the prospect of worse further difficulty if I should try to write an account of him and of our relationship—perhaps just to tire me out, wear me down; and to disgust me with the way I have been trying to live, trying to work and play at the same time, trying to love and not love at the same time. And to warn me of the terrible virtuosity and versatility and malleability of my imagination: my ability of disillusion with myself about no matter what in an instant, by one flourish of my hot spirit, one ejaculation of my sour wit; and my ability to embellish and dignify and even deify no matter who, for a while . . .

So I sat there more quietly gazing at my more or less deified fellow, Maine Priapus, Maine Proteus, over our two foamy beakers of ice cream, across the sticky little drugstore table of imitation onyx. And I felt sure that in any case our twenty-four hour intimacy had been somehow a terminal rather than an initiatory or inaugurative experience. It marked the end, not the beginning of a bizarre chapter of myself; the signal to give up as a bad job one of my methods of managing my wretched temperament. No doubt I should not have been thinking of a written account of it, if it were not so. There probably would not be many more such fellows in my life; anyway my approach to them, my hail and farewell to them, would never be the same. And the expression on my face as I thought of this must have been terrible. For at last my poor Hawthorn seemed really respectful of me; he shut up, and ceased winking and grinning at me. He looked not at all extraordinary, not superhuman or sub-human; he was just an ordinary lonesome small town New Englander like his friend at the soda fountain or like his ex-darling with too few teeth.

Finally one of the thunderstorms hanging all around struck Clamariscassett, softly flashing, rumbling, and with thick tepid drops; and with it the bus arrived; and I clambered up into it. As I sat there waving goodbye to Hawthorn through the drenched window I observed that—so long and laborious had our night together been, our sensational and enjoyable but not joyous intercourse—one of my elbows had been chafed by the sheet under us until it had drawn blood. How extraordinary! And so I departed, somewhat smiling at this silly indecent valedictory idea; how much tougher his sex had proved than my elbow! Also I sillily wondered if in the figurative and spiritual sense I could call myself thin-skinned; and in spite of my various excitability, I thought not. In any case, I mend, I mend, I mend!—as fast as any young warrior or any incorrigible old tomcat.

Violent showers overtook us every few miles all the way to Ellsworth. At one point for half an hour we rode under a canopy of ashen and bluish cloud, trimmed with long funereal ostrich. Behind us in the west this rich drapery swung apart, constituting a great oblong window, through which we looked miles away to a very different skyscape, all summery azure, upon which rested a flock of diminutive cirrocumulus, lamblike. And diagonally across the window, in front of the idyllic distance, there hung the voile of the rain in perfect little pleats.

Western skies are shinier, Mediterranean skies bluer; the characteristic thing about the Maine sky is its brilliance in a modest or intermediary or composite color: *grisaille*. Holland's in summer is like it, but less brilliant. The landscape also lends itself remarkably to strange light-effects. For there are almost no altitudes important enough or abrupt enough to wall one in; therefore the vistas are great, and as the road twines along the shore like a vine, they keep changing. Rock somewhat like alabaster and burnished hayfields and white architecture bend all along and baroquely frame the various bays and estuaries: ancient valleys submerged as the continent has tilted eastward; riverbeds flooded at whatever hour the moon has charmed the ocean. From these waters embedded in the countryside like looking-glass, an extraordinary cold refraction is always added to the sunlight; and a luxurious grayness like moonlight, ten times as strong, arises wherever the sun goes under a cloud.

Preoccupied with all this and the like, thus I returned from my escapade, to all intents and purposes delighted. I tried to make a few notes, to devise a few exact images, with my notebook on my jolted knees, my pencil jumping in my fingers. For the bus was traveling as fast as ever; the narrow highway was slippery; wind and showers kept rapidly and dimly enwrapping everything; now and then a little lightning snapped at us: it was fearful. The bus driver had struck up acquaintance with a pretty trained nurse in the seat next to his, somewhat behind him; so there was a good deal of turning of his head and rolling of his eyes away from the road, with modestly concupiscent small-talk. I could see that it was all a kind of playacting, foolishness; she would not see him again, and he knew it. It might have been the death of us nevertheless.

But now I felt no fear: to that extent at least love had had an improving effect upon me. Properly speaking, of course, there had not been the least love about it. Love had nothing to do with it. I did not care to see that poor Hawthorn again; I hoped and prayed that I might never need to see him: to that extent the present need had been attended to. Month after month I appear to be living under an evil spell of chastity cast by Monroe and George, those two who need me most and whom I love best. Last night's exercise had enabled me to feel that it was not necessarily so. It had cured me for a while of being sorry for myself. It had cleared my imagination of the temptations like a sideshow, the nightmare as sad as Saint Anthony's, by which for lack of love it gets naturally inhabited. Now in my early middle age, these three little changes of state of mind constitute what I am willing to call happiness: which is the best excuse I can give for bad sexy behavior. I know that my life is a wonderfully fortunate one, but I cannot always be glad of it. Often, when I am chaste, I cannot be glad of it. I know that my maker, so to speak, made me wonderfully well; but I am often unable to feel any gratitude. I am ashamed of this; and in the vagueness and hypochondria of shame everything goes wrong or seems to go wrong or seems very like to go wrong. But now, as a result of just a little bout of disgraceful forni-cation, for the time being I felt willing to call myself happy, willing to be myself, glad to be myself, able to face my maker without grimacing—that is, in a fit state to die. How fantastic and wonderful! And readiness to die is equivalent to courage: therefore I did not mind how foolishly the bus driver flirted, how damnably he drove, all the way to Sorrento.

The Stallions

Pages from an Unfinished Story

I live in an earthly paradise. The moodiest heat, and the duskiest rain, descending from soft blackish clouds hanging all along the eastern horizon. Flora of all sorts very noticeably, between one glance and the next, swelling and opening. In the hedgerow an old stub of peach tree that, to my knowledge, has never blossomed, blossoming. Over the outspoken brook, forsythia casting its harsh light, chemical yellow. The large petals of the magnolia standing up stiff against the cloudy horizon; flesh-pink, no, flesh-ruddy, against the vaporous black.

It happened that I had never seen the intercourse of mare and stallion. Horses are said to be nobler in their excitement than other animals, and less incomprehensible, that is to say less inhuman. I spoke of this to my brother a week or ten days ago, who laughed in his agreeable rustic tone and gazed at me fondly and expressed his surprise and regret. "But what a pity!" he said, "most of our mares are now in foal." Nevertheless, there was only a short wait before I could see two pairs of horses mate.

First there was the Suffolk stallion, Beauboy. One Saturday in the afternoon, while I sat beside Mother and Alexandra under a tree where a breeze was drawn, Saltmer the groom rode up on Beauboy— tiny Mediaeval-looking fellow with his legs split across the wide sleek back, barbet on charger. Alex went to consult him about black-smiths and veterinarians. I followed her and stood admiring the stallion: a ton of championship, a ton of potency, otherwise good for nothing. Tousled mane and forelock like a Louis-Quatorze wig; great scrotum of featherweight velvet; very dark wrinkles up and down his neck forming a great fan or shell whenever he looked over his shoulder.

I suppose the horse, as a symbol or ideal, in whatever connection, is always as foolish as this image of mine: supernal, impracticable. (Perhaps other *chefs-d'oeuvres* of nature likewise . . .) For a horse is always in a way, to a certain extent, insane. Its passions—like libido or gluttony or fright—possess it. For example, it is afraid of its rider, although at any moment it could kill him. On the other hand its love of its rider is not to be depended on, for it may kill him in a panic or by mistake. It fears fire terribly, but therefore does not flee from but remains amid the flames. It never knows enough not to eat itself to death, which, I have heard, is why it is not found as a wild animal in lands where the primeval pasture is rich. It learns almost nothing, that is, what it can be taught is nothing compared with what it is born knowing, born to do. How ludicrous and sad, its performance to music in fact; the quadruped Isadora, Nijinski of nature, keeps time less well than any rheumatic old person, tight, in a night club.

Then I heard either Alex or the groom say that Father had gone after Sapphire, the youngest imported mare.

Beauboy gazed with melancholy fondness afar across the meadow, where indeed there were mares, half a dozen as brilliant as a basketful of oranges overturned on the hot grass; and he called to them mistakenly. But now there came Father with the one in heat.

I must have been begotten with some such forceful flourish as Beauboy's, in a similar dumbness and somber delight. However, as my father approached with the young mare from the stable I was rather struck and touched by the dissimilarity between stallion and man. One human shoulder was stooped, the other lifted in a shrug; one paternal eye looked almost absent-minded, and he took the oddest, softest steps—formal as a pallbearer but absurdly sad, sad as a clown.

Father led Sapphire at a very prompt but weak trot around the big corncrib, inside the trail-gate. Meanwhile the groom allowed Beauboy to cavort around, immensely, cheerfully, expressing his interest with ardent nods, giant dance-steps. Then he put his penis out, a clumsy, limber sort of lance; and now and then he shook it erect, that is, straightened it up along his belly.

Alex remarked that evidently he was happy to have this young Sapphire. They have had a little trouble with him. The ninth day after delivering is the surest time for impregnation; but he does not care for mares who have lately foaled, who perhaps smell of blood and milk as well as uterus.

Also, I must say, I instantly thought up and slightly entertained this and that impure fantasy about it; fragment of indecent dream hurrying dimly on in my head and in some impossible direction, which now half recurs as I write. But the reality went so hurriedly and was so beautiful that nothing of the fanciful order counted or could count much.

In my retrospect I find this odd impression, pure enough: it was like Uccello, the master of the field of San Romano, those fringed uplifted hoofs and even that blackish lance were like that! The visual department of my mind, eager to preserve every one of the eye's snapshots, has done it repetitiously, criss-cross, like a battle scene, with difficult forms, attitudes overlapping, and many, many black lances. There too was the Florentine color: weedy green, woody red, and soiled shadow on the white wall of the corncrib. And Father's face and the groom's looked somehow dangerous and afraid at the same time; yes, it is a fact, they looked like condottieri, mercenary soldiers of old.

Now Saltmer the groom as well as Father was making a strange face, which reminded me of the mask of a clown, a clown of the sad sort, one of the Fratellinis as I remember them: abnormally calm, concentrating; no doubt it would have seemed to himself or anyone of his class a very proper, necessary face to make, in the way of the sorrowfulness of a remote relation at a funeral, complacent and a bit stylized. If he had been asked what he was feeling, no doubt he would have said that it was modesty, just modesty; he too was somewhat offended by his employer's wife's presence. But I am sure that it really amounted to more than that: it was the slightest instant of the greatest dizziness of instinct now and then, almost imperceptible, as it were a mote suddenly floating down across his attentive blue eye; it was the softest pang of the great pinch of pleasure. A delicate little fellow, in poor health; but he too is a very male man, with half a dozen children, one of them ill. Now and then he would take the stallion's troublesome reins in one hand, and with the other just touch his shoulder or the back of his neck oddly, as if he were being tickled.

First the stallion must ask the mare's permission which is almost invariably by biting. If she is not exactly ready for him, her womb not ripe, she will kick. The purpose of the trail-gate, behind which the mare waits, is to keep the stallion out of harm's way. Certain young males, such as Guardian, Beauboy's present coadjutor and rival—as if scarcely knowing how to distinguish between fornication and fighting—bite wickedly, no matter how or where, deserving to be kicked. Obviously old Beauboy knew better; he ran no risk, wasted no time. He stepped up slowly, not too close, stooping his heavy crest as elegantly as any swan, and he chose not Sapphire's throat or withers but a place just in front of the stifle-joint—a place where eleven month's hence the get of this intercourse (if it took effect) would rub its infant head as it groped her for milk—and a little of the lap of skin connecting the belly and the leg. And he very slowly disturbed these parts with his lips, with his hot nostrils, and then nipped: which was not much more severe than a man's kiss. Ripe young Sapphire permitted herself only a faint shiver, stupid, ready.

Beauboy having done his biting successfully, Saltmer said to Father in an earnest tone, "Lead her up that way," rapidly waving his little hand up that way; and Father did so. I had a moment of absurd anxiety, lest, where I stood, I should be unable to see the detail of the coupling, the wielding and hiding and showing of the male organ, and the receptivity of the female. It was all right; I could see.

Then Beauboy, with the groom hopping childishly alongside, flung himself forward to Sapphire, rearing a little at each step; and at the same time held up his penis, clenched it, as you might clench your fist for a fight, drew it, as you might draw a great crudely whittled arrow against a bow, then reared almost straight up the moment he reached her, and dropped his terrible forelegs over her back. Then, probably because I could no longer look at anything but the main thing, it seemed to me that the great phallus took charge of its operation itself; it seemed that it could not only feel but practically see, with its slant eye which soon, soon would weep; it seemed that it knowingly worked its way through the troublesome wrinkled lips, skillfully, as though sending a rocket, aiming at a target.

He must have given her eight or ten strokes, no, not that many; strokes perhaps two feet long, no, not that long. For in his strange striding position he was able to use only half to two-thirds of his penis. In the fine rosy part open like a wound between Sapphire's rust-red hindquarters surely there was more room than he needed. Also, first and last, there was more convulsion of his whole body than necessary, and not enough contact with her body, not enough correspondence and amalgamation—rapid straight strokes, with only the slightest variation or vibration, only a split second's pause and scarcely any urging at the end of each.

How else can I describe it? Indeed it is foolishness to try. It was as if simply, far up in the mare's placid wide-open body, there had been put a target which it was the stallion's game to aim at, and with difficulty to reach, and to strike a few times.

Whereas human intercourse is all rather superficial, that is, near the surface, and it is all rather patient, painstaking; the male as well as the female is patient, on purpose. Human intercourse is a stubborn, clasping and careful stretching and friction verging upon pain; all in detail, a detailed fondling, rubbing, massaging. The human purpose is to feel; the animal, to finish. Human intercourse is a shivering and making the other shiver until at last, verging upon exhaustion, worse comes to worst, which is our felicity. For us there does not seem to be any target; there should be no hurry. Whatever our hurry, it is like wrestling rather than this boxing, jabbing, stabbing.

Meanwhile, I wasted precious instants confusedly thinking of human passion.

Beauboy had his equine way; the dying of his desire and shedding of his sperm started. He did not clench his hoofs upon her flank as we do our fingernails; they hung loosely. He did not try to look at her as we try, amid little syncopes and darknesses, but faced the air over his head in a quite general, lonely fury. There could be only one more stab now. A terribly heavy horse, not a young horse, and generally an idle one, except when this happens; yet he stood almost straight up for it, like a monster bird about to take flight, with invisible wings: Pegasus.

Still, there was no semblance of unification, fusion. Think how human couples become an insoluble knot, irreparable puzzle! Nothing seemed to fit or to be quite fitting. He was still rather behind than upon her, so that it might have been a punishment, a flogging, a clubbing. Or an exploit: it might have been that he wished to lift her off the ground, spitted, for the fun of it.

That was the end. With his disheveled locks shaken above his old eyes of folly, he reminded me of King Lear. That was when it happened, that shudder of a harmless madness, of enough of immortality—who does not know it? It passed all through him, that is, it passed in its liquid form out of him. Whereupon great stallion like mere weak man apparently swooned.

"The wonder is that Sapphire can bear his weight," I murmured to my sister-in-law.

"It is all she can do. See the pitch of her poor quarters," she murmured back.

Beauboy's swoon was the finest thing of all to see. The terrible forelegs clasped her now, not in tenderness but to keep from falling. His head came down on one side, with pale eyes and waxen winded lips; and his flanks drew in and his withers stuck out; thus he stayed for a minute, like a huge shaken question mark. Then suddenly, in the small of his back which was driving his sex home, suddenly softness showed, and it spread upward, up his back and along his crest, and downward, down his legs, until he was apparently all soft and due to fall, but still not falling. This look of weakness impressed me as truly a look of strength, greater than I have ever seen before. The very idea that, when he looked so weak, still he should be able to hold up the ton or more of himself, precariously straining, upon half the feet that the engineering of nature has provided for it, until the end.

☙

Another day, one of our mares was mated with a neighbor's Arab stallion. Ibn-Nafa is not a young horse, and he is as lean as if he still had to live on the dew and sprigs in his arid fatherland. His limbs are as slender as a Greyhound's and the torso is extraordinarily cut out around them, in what you might call the equine armpit and equine groin. He holds his head in an intense crook like the hippocampus of Greek mythology. He is startlingly beautiful. A beauty which is all expression and animation: expression very dramatic and movement very rhythmic.

When finally he saw Winona, dark, musing, held by Saltmer, there among the apple trees, he promptly adjusted his mood to what, after all, was expected of him. There was no trail-gate; she had been teased by Beauboy or Guardian before leaving home. Ibn-Nafa went straight toward her as if his master had also assured him of it in so many words: all set, go on, she will not kick. This hoofed Escudero reached his female somewhat at an angle, and mounted so. There was very little toiling or delving, very little piston motion; but on the other hand the easy-seeming ejaculation went on a long time, they lightly swaying together as if in a far-away waltz.

When we got home and put Winona in her stall with her colt Mecca, he too behaved fantastically. He is the prettiest baby-beast on earth, we think: with every muscle as smooth as fruit, every tendon impeccable, and wild-looking crescent ears, and a blaze like an exclamation point. Now he is shedding his infant fuzz; under the golden chestnut of that, the color he will be, a sort of midnight brown, shows in streaks. He's just two months old. Yet his mother's return from his father's embrace meant all the world to him. Having snuffed up and down her tail a while, delighting in their mixed fragrance, he thrust out his infant penis and held it straight and sharp, and so went prancing all around her and, with tosses of his exquisite head, kept looking up at her back as if only their differences in height restrained him from incest. The Arab is a famously amorous horse, more so than the noble Suffolk or coarse Belgian. And I suppose that in general, where sex appears greatest, in ostentatious embodiment or personification, it is not strongest. Idea and ideal and affection are the great hormones.

The Frenchman Six Feet Three

Roger Gaumond when I first knew him was wonderfully hand-some. He had one of those faces reminiscent of a young Roman of the decline and fall, a good-natured Antonine or a grand-bourgeois Antinous. But even then people laughed at him because, for a Parisian, he was huge. He was six feet two or three, with stat-uesque shoulders, and ideal hands which got in the way, and feet like a pedestal. He had attractive blue eyes in which there was a sparkle of worry, and he was blond with very white skin. I remember that perspiration would appear on his noble forehead if he got into the least emotion or effort, and a good many things made him blush. When I was last in France—in 1938—he had begun to look some-what gross and sad. His grandeur inclined to be fat, his pallor had turned sallow, and there was something spoiled about his romantic mouth.

He was the sole son and heir of a well-known family of the more or less grand middle class, with money. His father was an industrialist of consequence, and he himself had a good position in a small manufactory on the left bank of the Seine beyond Sèvres in which his grandmother and one of his great-aunts had a controlling interest. I think he did not care much about his work except for the remunera-tion of it. He never complained, he rarely made any reference to it at all. He lived by himself in a pleasant apartment in the Rue Constant, in the aristocratic *arrondissement* of Paris, that is, the seventh. He cared about old furniture, at least to the extent of furnishing his rooms painstakingly and as nobly as he could afford. He also owned a little house outside Paris, at La Miel in the valley of the Chevreuse, where he spent certain months in the spring and summer, driving to work and back in a small but elegant Buick. He enjoyed gardening, priding himself almost boringly upon the special seeds and foreign bulbs which he was able to bring to bloom at La Miel amid his quincunx of apple trees.

He loved music more than all else, particularly Mozart and Wagner, traveling annually to Salzburg and Bayreuth for the *Festspiele*. In the past ten years, year after year, he had come home with an unhappy appreciation of the efficacy of the new German state and the might of the modernized German army. Even in 1938 you risked being called pro-Nazi if you prophesied too well in that way; and some of his friends, especially British and Americans, did call him one. He simply said that it was disgusting of them. I think he felt so absolutely part and parcel of his native land that it would not have occurred to him that his patriotism could be doubted, except as a joke, and a joke in bad taste furthermore.

He was an odd inexpressive fellow. He kept the life of his senses a mystery, a mystery to me at least. His life of the spirit seemed all concentrated in a certain cool, habitual, and often grumbling friendliness toward such Americans as Linda Brewer and myself, and certain cousins of his who lived in Versailles, and especially toward a good scholarly fellow named Alain Raffe. Both Roger and Alain Raffe were quite happy young men, I believe; but somehow the expression of displeasure and unhappiness seemed to come more naturally to them than any enthusiasm, and in their general view of life perhaps they never really expected anything very good to last very long.

While I was in Paris that spring of 1938 Roger was summoned to do reserve military service for a fortnight. He had been told that it would be in some portion of the Maginot Line, somewhere between Metz and Sedan. This stirred my curiosity or my imagination, no doubt because I have found the martial architecture of France wonderfully satisfactory to my aesthetic sense, more so in many ways than the ecclesiastical or the residential—especially the works of Vauban, and little Aiguesmortes like a lily with open calyx and pistil and stamens of stone, and that star of masonry lying on the shore at Antibes and great theatrical Pierrefonds. Multiply all that by hundreds of miles, adorn it with the obscurest modern inventions, I imagined, and you would have the Maginot Line. Sometimes indeed I will catch myself daydreaming of France as having something of that kind upon its borders: edifices brooding distantly in the dull landscape of the departments of the East and Northeast, a battlement as permanent as the Pyramids.

Roger, I must say, when he was called up did not seem inspired by any such mental picture. A little tartly he suggested that, for him, the fortnight ahead meant having to work like a dog in a place probably like a cellar; and in fact, in general, for all concerned, national defense must be a matter of working like dogs, not of a taste for austere architecture.

He asked Alain and me to dine with him the night of his departure for those famed bastions. He had to take an early train, so he suggested our coming to the Rue Constant in the late afternoon for a drink and a farewell chat. His apartment was in one wing of what had been in the great past a ducal palace, overlooking a garden. There were platbands in which the spring flowers were green but had not yet begun to blossom; and there was a little lineup of trees under Roger's window leading back to a fine small rococo pavilion occupied by his landlady, who was a cabinet minister's widow.

While we drank and chattered we helped Roger into his uniform, which had been sent to his apartment for him to depart in. And when I say we helped, it is not just in a manner of speaking. For it was too small for him by some four or five inches in every dimension. His long and not very muscular forearms as well as his blue-veined wrists and white hands protruded out of the sleeves of the faded blue tunic. Between the tops of the boots and the bottoms of the breeches there were absurd extents of calf over which we had to wind the puttees with the greatest care, securing them with safety pins. Happily, the boots themselves were roomier than the other items, and by leaving them unlaced, resigning himself to certain blisters, he was able to walk well enough, clumpingly. The exiguity of the topcoat did not matter; he would carry it over his arm. The exiguity of the breeches was the real hardship, which could not be helped. They bifurcated him within an inch of his life; and there was real reason to fear a giving-away in the seat or somewhere if he made any sudden motion.

At first all this seemed to amuse Roger, but by the time we had completed him as a military man he had begun to take a dark view. "How sad this is," he exclaimed, in those tenor tones which they use in France when things go wrong. "How they have made me ridiculous! How idiotic it is!"

Then, sore-footedly and with grotesque precaution, he practiced walking up and down his fine salon. He had furnished it with a variety of old beauty, very fine: black and brass cabinets of the great century—that is, the seventeenth—and a bronze bust and a good gilt clock and ancestral curtains; and it had an ornately inlaid old floor. It was a strange sight, I thought—the huge improvised soldier in the peaceful setting, in his garb of war so poverty-stricken, stricken and cramped, skidding a little on the beautifully waxed wood. It was very funny, though now naturally it does not seem so.

He strode, if in breeches so uneasy it could be called striding, across to one of the tall windows and he gazed into the garden. "It's sickening! It's idiotic!" he said again.

Then he remarked that he was ashamed to be caught in this disgraceful typical national plight by an efficient American like myself: limping off to one's military service, trussed up in someone else's pants! I reminded him not to be too sure of America's efficiency. I stood there at the window for a moment gazing into the garden with him. There was a flicker of candles in the great political widow's windows; she had guests. In the six o'clock light the gravel of the path past Roger's wing to her door looked like seed pearls. There was a cool breeze coming up as the evening fell, and the short green ribbons of young narcissus waved in the angular flowerbeds along the path. "How pretty it is, don't you think?" said Roger.

After dinner we accompanied him to the Gare de l'Est. French railway terminals are all somewhat alike, I suppose, and surely the Gare de l'Est is not the largest and shabbiest, but that night it seemed so. It had an atmosphere of limbo, it was as cold as limbo.

There were hundreds of friends and relatives saying goodbye on the platform, a long rough fringe of average humanity all along the train that poor Roger had to take. Having been away from France for years, I was affected by this crowd as if it had been music, memory-laden and homesick. Indeed it was not my home but it was a place wound into my thought and my senses too closely, too long, ever to be unwound or forgotten. I had not forgotten the particular body odor of Frenchmen in a mass like this, rather like a vaseful of stale carnations, it seemed to me; carnations and a little garlic. I noted once more how many of their commonest faces have visionary eyes and, once more, I was made uncomfortable by their jostling which is less innocent and friendly than the American way but no less democratic.

Until the whistle of departure blew, some young men with their darlings and a few couples probably married kept embracing as it is done in France, face to face, with their arms round each other rather low, clasped in the small of each other's back. Now and then they took deliberate kisses and then seemed to be brooding separately on love, each staring up and straight ahead over the beloved's shoulder.

There were as many mothers as wives and sweethearts; and when the whistle finally blew, peep peep, all this female assembly, maternal and enamored alike, suddenly appeared to sag and shrink, left behind together, deprived of their chief interest, their fond hearts without focus. It changed the physical aspect of the crowd a little all the way down the platform.

It was a long train composed of those small wooden coaches which are a peculiarity of France, like little old chicken coops on wheels. I was pleased to see that Roger, the giant, could indeed stand up inside one, but in order to talk to us from the window of his compartment he had to stand with his legs bent, his tight shoulders more than ever like those of Atlas, with a world of self-pity and sophisticated sense of humor on them.

Peep, peep, and the long lightweight train, low on its wheels, slid out into the dark, eastward. And then a hundred hands were flung up, very white; even the grimy hands looked white in the weak illumination of the train shed. It was one long flutter of farewell so intense that it was rather like a desperate beckoning to come back.

Of course there is great love everywhere in the world, and the abuse and defrauding of pleasure everywhere. But France was the place, I suppose, where the average man and woman got the most out of their faculties of love. In this way and in their close family ties they probably always have been more vulnerable than other nations. Now indeed it is obvious how bad for them it must be to have a couple of million of their men in the prime of life kidnapped and kept away; the best breeding stock of the country rounded up behind barbed wire. That was one thing which in my darkest sensibility to Europe in 1938 I did not anticipate. Yet this departure of men, this farewell of women, seemed to me almost sinister. I knew that men departing to military service were the hope of France; one hope of the whole world for that matter. I really had no reason to fret about them except that their raiment and paraphernalia and even the coaches in which they traveled looked a hundred years old.

When Roger returned two weeks later it was near the end of my European holiday, and engagements and errands had so entangled me that I had to put off seeing him. Then he invited me to spend a day at La Miel, which I did, on the second, or perhaps the third, Sunday in April. I had tired myself out in certain difficult intimacies in Paris, and was in a mood to be amused by such a careless companion as Roger; and furthermore Linda Brewer also had a house in La Miel. She is a really old and fond friend of mine, one of my generation, a fellow-writer whom I really admire, not a novelist but a journalist in the great way, personal, unpretentious, and scrupulous, which I admire almost as much as the art of the novel. As she had a better judgment of the French, and a more courageous prophetic feeling for entire Europe, than anyone else I knew, I wanted to see her once more before I returned to our country.

She had a stint of writing to do that Sunday, so she could not invite us to lunch. Roger and Alain Raffe and I spent all the middle of the day outdoors; Roger at work in his garden with a serious breathlessness and an earnest account of the why and wherefore of everything, Alain and I pretending to work and to listen. For two weeks I had been thinking of Roger as deep down inside the mysterious Line, in a labyrinth, in a cellar. It surprised me to find him a little tanned or at least weathered. He looked well. Now he was taking an almost gluttonous pleasure in his flower beds, kneeling and crawling, poring over every infant bit of green, plunging his hands out of sight into the mulch and the soft dry sifted soil.

I had no spirit to gossip, I could not listen, I could scarcely think, in a spell of the admiration and melancholy of France, now that I was about to leave it again. Over Roger's low orchard walls one could gaze a long way into the valley of the Chevreuse, a landscape with no flatnesses, with no heights, with scarcely any character except its mere attractiveness. The sunshine was so clear, the blue of the sky so sharp, that the earth seemed lacking in color. For several kilometers around it looked like a drawing in pastel, with the color a little rubbed off or blown away from the design, and some color blowing powdery in the air, in the breeze. The breeze was what they call a wind in France, and it had been so for almost a month, with extraordinary brilliance day after day, and drought and quite cold nights. It was a bad spring for fruit trees. Even Roger's sheltered and rugged apple trees were affected, blooming now with what was rather like a bud broken open than a proper blossom, and the brownish pink of the petals indicated that they would open no farther. But all the milky sweet-sourness peculiar to apple blossom exhaled down the heavy branches, in which bees were working stubbornly, reeling and blundering in the bad energy of the air.

About four o'clock we strolled over to Linda's for tea and sandwiches and whiskey. It was chilly then, and our tired Frenchmen were glad to sit by the fire with Mrs. Lavery, the beautiful friend with whom Linda lived. Linda and I sat by ourselves on the far side of the room and talked our politics, international politics—Great Britain and America, America and France, France and Germany—with a certain wisdom, I do believe, relatively speaking, though surely we were unpretentious enough about that. We were quite honest in our narrow hopes and great general dread; no doubt we were very clever, and we felt that we were intelligent, but we did not pretend to be wise, even to each other.

We have in common—at least we have together—moods of an odd combination of unashamed sentiment with some toughness or hardness. And now little by little, in allusions amid what we had to say about politics, we were bidding each other an extraordinarily fond and significant kind of farewell. "When are you sailing?" she asked, and I told her.

"You know, you're quite right not to stay here," she said. "No one is going to be able to write fiction in France from now on. Do you think you will be able to, even at home, when the war gets going? Oh, I wish I could go home with you! How I envy you, in a way."

But she corrected herself. She did not envy me, she said; it was only her sentimentality and imagination. To stay in France as long as it was humanly possible was her fate. Because it was fate of course she herself did not altogether understand why it was. "But I shall be the last to leave. The last Middle-Westerner on this peninsula of Europe, of Eurasia."

I approved of her staying. If she must she must, I said. But then I rather made fun of her or, you might say, fun of the evil fate coming up to engulf perhaps everyone on earth. "Don't be too brave, don't stay too long. You will be a great nuisance to us."

"Why?"

"We'll have to come and rescue you. We'll have to send a destroyer to get you. We'll find you in the fog on the sands at the foot of the Phare d'Quessant, or up on one of those crazy pinnacles of the Finistère coast, waving your silk handkerchief. We'll take you off the rocks in a breeches-buoy."

I thought it a good joke in my way, a pretty scene, and it still sticks in my imagination: one of those inlets or coves of a matchless crazy beauty in Finistère, a dead extremity of the body of Europe, a broken tip of the index finger of Eurasia. There is a seashore of dead-white stone which the ocean has half eaten; it is as if a cave had opened and its stalagmites had come out and were standing about. There are enormous skulls of the stone lying there and the ocean keeps cleaving them open, pulling the teeth and washing the sinuses, and the wind meanwhile preys upon the ocean, goring and sawing it and gagging it and hurling it into the stalagmites and the skulls, with its gray blood and disgusting spit spattering in the air for kilometers inland. It is one of those scenes which are impressive because they are reminiscent of human passion at its bitterest, of human physiology at its hardest, of starvation and sex and surgery and the like; but amid which actually a human being looks and feels as minute and shabby and functionless as a trained flea, badly trained at that!

"You have powerful friends, dear," I told Linda. "And you're worth a destroyer."

I have a loud voice, and across the room Roger and Alain and Mrs. Lavery heard this. They sighed and shrugged and smiled, probably regarding us in spite of affection as persons of excessive fantasy and wild talk. Just then Linda's old housekeeper entered with the tea and whiskey and bread and cheese, and we moved over to the fireside.

"I wish we were powerful," Linda said. "We," she insisted, with emphasis on the first person plural, "are not powerful."

It charmed me to find on the tea-table a poor old copy of *The Methodist Hymnal*, the earliest book of my life except perhaps *The Wizard of Oz*. Linda had bought it for five francs from a stall on the Quai Voltaire and had just been looking in it for a quotation. It started us talking of the great moral effects of congregational singing, Catholic versus Protestant, and then we spoke of national anthems. Mrs. Lavery was a musician, a lifelong student and practicer of singing who intended to make a career of it. The month before last she had been engaged to sing our excessively difficult "Star-Spangled Banner" at a Washington's Birthday banquet.

Meanwhile I had been turning the pages of the hymnal, with pleasure and almost pathetic reminiscence of my Wisconsin childhood. Thanks to my mother's teaching and devout influence, this kind of simple Protestant music is second nature for me. I told Linda and the others how, as a boy soprano with high notes like those of a strained flute, I was sometimes paid as much as three dollars to sing at funerals, standing beside the coffins in little country parlors fumigated with tuberoses. It impressed them. Then I suggested our singing a few hymns. Roger and Alain refused but Linda and Mrs. Lavery were charmed to.

The latter had a fine high voice, trained as the French train their singers especially for the German repertory, with a golden tubular tone. The difficulty for her seemed to be that her exquisite physique was not stalwart enough for the volume of sound she had learned to produce. It made her pretty neck, which was like a water bird's, throb, and the note would slip. I played the piano. Linda sang now the alto, now the tenor notes.

I love looking at Linda when she talks, as I think everyone does; and there is much the same charm when she sings. She is not what is called a pretty woman; all her features, her nose, her brow, her lips, are somewhat too strong or too distinctive. And when she is silent you can see how her spirit and excess of expressions have aged her face, a little in anticipation or in advance of the way she will look in due time anyway. As it is, I think her appearance is not likely to change much as she grows older. I regard her as fairly typical of our generation of emancipated, vagabond, international American, with a naturally worried mind but never discouraged in the least, cynical but conscientious—a pleasant enigma to most Europeans. Sometimes, when the matter of her talk or her thought is unhappy she has a look of almost ugly indignation. Then in the other extreme, her good humor will turn to a kind of wildness and glee which is extraordinary, like a Greek mask. She dresses her hair in a lovely rough bob all round her head; it is gray hair, filaments of iron or spun ashes. In those old days in France she wore a monocle.

To sing, she put in her monocle and held her head a little to one side. We sang Watts' "Man Frail and God Eternal," most appropriate: "Like flowery fields the nations"—that is, I thought, the democracies—"stand, pleased with the morning light." We sang poor insane William Cowper's "God moves in a mysterious way, His wonders to perform." We sang "Joy to the world," to Handel's tune, which would have made a better national anthem than the one we have.

I happened to look up over the grand piano and observed that our Frenchmen could scarcely bear it. Their large figures were slumping in their armchairs. Their faces, in the mixed daylight and firelight, showed no more animation than a pair of carvings in white wood. It was as if all feeling had moved out of them somewhere else, as if their hearts had fled, because it had become intolerable to feel anything, in proximity or in conjunction with whatever it was they were thinking. They were both Roman Catholics, although neither of them professed any belief. Perhaps the hue and cry we made was hard for them in the theological sense. We were real American Protestant-pagans, all three of us.

Upon second thought I suppose it was the matter of nationality rather than the matter of faith. Superior French of the class and schooling of Roger and Alain do often regard us as not quite civilized people, which does not hinder them from generally liking us. Roger and Alain particularly liked us three and must have assumed that we were a good deal less than one hundred percent American. But there we were, with loud united voice and absent united mind, unabashed, absorbed in a native Sunday-afternoon ceremony. As it must have struck them, this was the old Adam coming out in us too, the old American Adam. We were powerful, we were happy, and furthermore, we were somewhat outside civilized history; and they loved us; and presently we would withdraw from them in fact as well as in spirit. Heathenish and cold-blooded and heartbreaking, we doubtless would go away and leave them.

Then Linda had to do some more work and it was time for us to dine, so we returned to Roger's. Alain, who was expecting a long-distance call from his father in Brussels, hastened on ahead. It was a cold twilight with a great fragrance, particularly that fermenty fragrance of sod which has lately been frozen or frosted. There was an afterglow folded in cloud. We strolled down a narrow old lover's lane, under trees preserved in loving-kindness to a great age, then along a field of little vines all nursed and cut and healed and kept in harness, then along a soft orderly brook, and across a meadow on a well-worn path. Suddenly huge Roger turned toward me and talked to me.

"Listen, Alwyn," he began. He said my peculiar name almost as if it were Hallowe'en without the H. He stood in the middle of the path and talked fast. "Listen, Alwyn, I must tell you this. I did not care to mention it in Linda's presence; she would think it a good thing to put in an article for *Harper's* or *The New Yorker*. And that would be worse than not telling it at all, because the men who are important never, on principle, believe a thing that they read in articles or in the newspapers. And there has been, my lord, enough of the shame of France. I am ashamed. I will not see any more of it in print. Not even abroad; not even when it is written by those like you and Linda who still feel that you are our allies. And, alas, if the Germans ever come to the conclusion about us that I've come to, God save us!

"I tell you this, Alwyn, because you must know some men who have power in New York and Washington. You can speak in our behalf, to impress upon them the necessity of helping us. Unless you stand by us we shall fail you. You cannot depend on us unless you help us."

"Roger," I interrupted sharply, "what are you talking about? What in the world is this?"

It was, as I might have guessed, the feebleness of the army of France, the inefficacy or ignorance of the government of France, the numerical if not personal inferiority of the French, the inadequacy of the heavy industry of France, the futility of the eastern and northeastern fortifications; in general, the hopeless imparity between the French and their enormous evil incomparable enemy. Roger had suspected all this for some time, and his two weeks' service in the Marginot Line had settled it for him.

"We are lost, we have not a hope, it is finished. France is past. Oh, God, I am so tired of thinking about it! How can we go to war, in the perfect certainty of defeat? What do the English expect of us? They despise us and yet they depend on us. When it is all over you will all say that we were cowards, crooks, degenerates, a nation of eunuchs. But how can we fight well when we have seen with our own eyes, to start with, that we have only old guns, little tanks, a few planes, and that crazy line of fortresses which the Germans understand perfectly, and not one of us has learned anything up to date, no one knows what to do?"

I could not exactly see Roger's face, in the double-focus light of the dusk, not night yet but nocturne. But I did not need to see it. I knew what expression of the idleness of grief it wore. Irritably, stubbornly, I began to assure him that his pessimism was not to be trusted and that, in him and others like him, it constituted a worse disadvantage to the Republic than the shortcomings which inspired it.

Unfortunately my heart was not altogether in what I said. For if, at any time during the past decade, I had been asked whether in my opinion France had a first-rate army, I should have answered no. This was of course nothing but an impression, based on casual glances into various casernes and camps; on long waits at street corners for certain parades to pass; on conversations with some young men, soldier boys or ex-soldier boys who did not mean to tell me anything in particular, who suffered from none of Roger's emotion.

As I remember, whenever you encountered the French army, there was a kind of gypsy atmosphere; it was agreeable, amiable. You saw as it were great untidy picnics of the military maneuvering along the roads, with the right idea and ideal surely, and businesslike in some ways, but with unbecoming uniforms and quaint-looking guns, with improvisation and patchwork. Inside aged masonry of a hundred traditional fortresses you could always discover something human, picaresque or idyllic or melancholy: little old temperamental mules, little old ardent officers, a mess table outdoors with fragrant soup in tin basins, a flutter of body linen drying on a clothesline. All over France you heard a bit of the music of the trumpet at dawn or at dusk, *divertimento*, as innocent, as rustic as a rooster crowing or a whippoorwill.

What Roger had to report, or rather to express, was a little worse than my impression; but probably that was because it meant more to him than to me. It was nothing very interesting, it was not news. He stood astride of the path waving his heavy arms, chattering rather than shouting. It was a mere outburst of simple conviction; refreshing in a sense, in France, where even in sadness there was usually too much moderateness and doubt. It was an outcry, an almost poetical generalization. His words themselves were flat and middle-class. A word here and there gave the idea, as in an opera, and the voice did the rest, that extraordinarily light voice, coming a little incongruously from the bulk of his shadowy figure in the empty meadow.

Really it amounted to nothing more than that the Maginot Line had been a bitter disappointment to him. He must have had false hopes of it after all, something like my dream of martial architecture which he had made fun of. In his actual report of his two weeks it was hard to tell exactly what was what; he had no reportorial talent. I wanted to inquire how long it had been before they had issued him a comfortable uniform, but he did not mention it and I was afraid of seeming to mock him. He did not really satisfy my curiosity in any respect. As I say, his mind was all lyricism and criticism. The Maginot Line has remained, to my mind, an enormity of mythical building with especially my Roger in it, my tragical, laughable giant talking so much and saying so little that was memorable or quotable.

He told me that officers were severe with the men, but ruefully, like doctors keeping some secret. The men were not insubordinate or even sullen. They were rather, as to the possibility of war before long, the limitations of their equipment, and their own shortcomings in the sense of aptitude for war and training for war, tactful with one another. None of them of course knew for a fact that their matériel was inferior to the enemy's, but all of them somehow had been given some suspicion of it. They respected one another, and they had self-respect; but as to the guns and shells and instruments and supplies they were working with, they had only a sense of humor. As it had seemed to Roger their good behavior itself, given all these implications, was ominous.

As French as can be, Roger then tried to explain the state of mind in the Line by referring to a book. "Have you read *Les Caves du Vatican?*" he asked.

I had indeed; it is André Gide's fantastic satire in which the Pope has been kidnapped and secretly imprisoned in the Vatican basement and an imposter has taken his place. Roger said that in the Line you kept thinking that there must be some supreme superior officer over all the other officers, and perhaps he was an imposter, perhaps he was deranged, perhaps he was a dead wraith. In any case the others did not understand the orders he gave, but as they re-gave them they pretended to.

The particular fortress to which Roger had been sent was an old building, built by the Germans in 1912 or 1913. When the victorious French recovered Alsace they found it in good condition and they economically incorporated it into their new battlements.

"The droll thing is," Roger said, "that we never troubled to remove the German signs painted up on the walls inside it here and there, over the doors, in the corridors. Signs like *Damen* and *Herren*, not really *Damen* and *Herren*; there were no *Damen* except in our dreams. All the other things to do and not to do, *Vorsicht, Stufe,* and *Rauchen und spucken streng untersagt,* for example. We left all that just as it was, in the messy, funny Gothic letters, to save money."

His accent in German was good and evidently it amused him to speak it. "All the *Achtungs,* and the *Tür unter keiner Bedingung zu öffnen,* and all the *Verbotens.* I tell you it had an effect of hallucination. It was a German fortress anyway, and sometimes when I was tired I fancied that we were Germans already and did not know it."

This made Roger laugh, and in laughter—as it often happens, praise God, in all sorts of human emergency—he suddenly began to recover his composure. We went on our way home then along the path. We found Alain playing the phonograph and we listened for a quarter of an hour. Then we dined, very leisurely and well; and after dinner we gossiped of indifferent acquaintances, certain musicians and the children of certain friends, and went early to bed.

A few days later, when I said goodbye to Roger for who knows how long or perhaps forever, I suddenly realized that I had scarcely any affection for him left. The drama of France was too great, and his personal unhappiness and indignation about it too small, small and abstract. He had a broken heart, which is a sick, stupid thing, I said to myself. As a rule those whose hearts are really broken may as well be given up as a bad job. Unless they are quite young, one can do nothing with them or for them. Roger was truly patriotic and perhaps truly sensitive to the future, yet I had an impression of laziness all woven in with his feeling. Certainly, I thought, there must have been something more to the point for him to do than to unburden himself to a mere vacationing American strolling across a crepuscular pasture upon an April evening in the valley of Chevreuse.

No doubt it was and still is foolish to judge France by men like my Roger, either in condemnation or in excuse. The man who makes an outcry is never quite the same as the inarticulate fellow-humanity behind him. And perhaps even my impatience with Roger individually was unjust. All over the world better men than he have done no more good than he; and the majority of good men did not even have his foresight and emotion.

I still wonder at the simplicity and the courage of the chiefs of state allied to France in basing their policy and strategy upon the military might of the French and the obscure fame of those battlements in Alsace. I suppose they never happened to meet any Rogers. I find it hard to believe that our brilliant American foreign correspondents, brave honest indefatigable fact-finders, never discovered that the French army would be good for nothing in a modern war. Probably they did discover everything, but, in their passionate devotion to the democratic cause, lest they discourage or demoralize their readers, kept imposing upon themselves a certain self-censorship. Now in New York I often discuss this with my friend Linda, but it is a mystery we cannot solve.

She was not in fact the last to leave France—far from it; no breeches-buoy! In May 1940 she came home, for a few weeks, as she thought, because her father was in danger of death; and meanwhile France surrendered and she could never get a passport to go back. The last we heard of Roger was that in June 1940 he was in some sector of the Maginot Line between Sedan and Metz, perhaps in that same fortress of the German inscriptions, *Vorsicht* and *Verboten*. That, as Linda reminded me the other day, was where the German army slipped through. So probably he is now behind barbed wire, or laboring as a slave upon a highway or an underground airport or some other wonderful project of enemy engineering. I like to think that, as his German is excellent and he loves Wagner and he is an amiable creature, he gets on well enough with his captors.

The Love of New York

What is the place to live? I have lived in fact, as most people do, hither and thither almost indifferently, wherever I could be near the one I loved, or where there appeared to be some economic advantage in my living, or where I expected to be able to work well. But what if I had not had these motives? If nothing mattered to me; if I had given my talent up as a bad job, and therefore no longer felt obliged to live in any particular place for a specific purpose; if I had fallen out of love and it was final, and no one, none of my family, none of my customary dear friends, needed me or wanted me anywhere; and if, with nothing but my own inclination to consider, I had my choice of the entire earth—where should I choose to spend the rest of my life? The answer is New York.

New York, for its own sake, rather than Rome or London or Paris, although it is a disadvantageous place in many ways. Society in it is almost all alcoholic, and there are not nearly enough servants who take any pride or pleasure in their work. It boasts of its modernity, but it is a vain boast while millions have to go on dwelling in built-over brownstones, heating themselves up something unappetizingly on gas rings stuck in cupboards amid ineradicable cockroaches; and it has other shames and shortcomings. It is uncomfortable and it is expensive. The chances are that whatever you have to live on, whatever you do for a living, would entitle you to a higher standard of living somewhere else.

It is not even, in the strict sense of the aesthetic of cities, very beautiful. Think of Paris and Rome and London. New York is in a different category. As it grew, so little of it was ever planned ahead of time, and so little handed down to us about it as preconceived or traditional, that we think of it rather as landscape than as human construction and habitation. To be sure, it was humanity which aligned it in cliffs, and cut its faded canyons, and lifted it up and pieced it together nest by nest, rough-and-tumble around the horizon. But it might have been accident, the elements, the tides, and stubborn running water; or the instinctive work of generations of birds. Look at it, as you cross on a ferry from one of the islands out in the harbor; it consists of large dark sticks stacked this way and that, amid large withered reeds lapped by the waves; and hearing its congested traffic squawking, you half-expect some great thing to be startled up out of it, flapping panicky wings. Look up, as you walk or taxi south through the park: what you see is a part of a mountainside, with the atmosphere wound across it in wild vines, and when the night falls, the profusion of electricity ripening all over it.

I think it is the only great city with all the importance and activity and amusement of city life, which nevertheless appeals to the imagination like wild country. Its charm depends on the weather, the light and dark, and the time of day, and the momentary emotion of the beholder. If we stop to consider it without emotion, or if we look too close, it is a disappointment; it is not at all according to human aestheticism or idealism. Like the wondrous works of God in nature, the other wondrous works of God in nature—glacier, jungle, flood, floor of the ocean—it is disorderly and unattractive in detail.

But we never care, having in mind a certain mirage to add to the reality; a visionary composite picture of it as a whole which makes us indifferent to any poor minor matter we may not like. The fact for us is continually mixed with what we have expected of it, and still expect. As one says promised land, it is promised city. It is as if we had journeyed to it from some other place—which indeed a good many of us have done—and come upon it suddenly and stood gazing starry-eyed, at some little distance, outside it looking in; and in a sense we have stayed outside. We still generally look at it as we did the first time, half in imagination, preferring our hope to our experience. An odd way to feel about a crowded, soiled, commercialized, mechanized cityscape.

The discoverers of this country when they first came must have had this kind of imagination about landscape, beginning with the sight of the coastline arising out of the abstract sea—blank beaches upon which there had been no footprints until they set foot, lonely beckoning rivers which had had no boats on them big enough to count until they sailed up—and the colonizers and gold-rushers had it, I suppose, wending their way with pack animals and folded camp up the long valleys toward palatial, perhaps golden foothills; and the pioneers had it, I know (because my grandparents told me), when deep amid the skyscraping primeval timber through the foliage they caught the first shimmer of some natural clearing. It was a daydream and it was their passion; and naturally they suffered a deep dread of disappointment, but they imagined that it offered them the greatest opportunity in the world; and they realized what that opportunity was going to do to them: it was going to take their all, whether or not it gave its all. Because it was their passion, they were willing. Which, I think, is the spirit of many New Yorkers about New York. For some of those forerunners of ours, and for some of us, who happen to have no deep amorous attachment, it takes the place of that in a sense. Also it bears a certain similarity to religion. They thought and spoke explicitly, and also sang about the religious aspect of their way of life and lifework, and we do not; but perhaps that does not make a great difference. A subconscious sentiment, passion, or superstition may have as much effect on one's conduct as any regular creed; nowadays, as a rule, it has much more effect.

New York, they say, is all things to all men; and as I give it so definite a character, perhaps I should specify and locate my part of it. A number of its parts, and provincial cities, grow close around it, attached to it, and each has some peculiarity and takes knowing: talented and feckless Harlem, the mysterious Bronx, combative Brooklyn, the salt-marsh cities of New Jersey, prepotent Astoria. I do not really love all those parts, I scarcely know them. The New York I mean is the center of town, mid-Manhattan, the important part. If anyone wanted to alter this country at one fell swoop, let us say by bombing, this would be the place to swoop. It is not large: an area of a square mile or so, the fifties between Fifth Avenue and Park Avenue, and a bit more. The true New Yorker cannot ever walk there without having to say how-do-you-do to people, as in a village; that in fact is how he knows that he is a true New Yorker. And he may fancy that he has nothing in common with his fellow how-do-you-doers except this habit of walking in certain blocks. What they have in common, really, is a lifework: the management, the promotion, the education, the re-creation, and the fashion of the place, by which the adjacent and provincial places are governed; and naturally their influence extends to the rest of the country as well, and now—as in convulsive history the planet shrinks—it has begun to be extended everywhere. The rest of the country could get on without them, of course, but then it would be, as you might say, automatic.

My own role is not historic; I am not one of the managerial class. All I can contribute to the great work and destiny of the metropolis is my contemplation of it and rejoicing in it, and when called upon, a certain testimony. And it is not always a joyous contemplation. In fact I think the bitterest sentiments I have ever had to endure have been various disappointments in New York. If I did not love it, I should hate it. I remember the day of my worst bitterness, a day in late December; and that same afternoon, walking in the street, between one errand and another, an odd thing happened to me. It was a sort of mystic experience.

Now mystic, I know, is a big word, too much in use and as a rule misused, and I suppose one ought not to write it any more without defining it. But it requires a long hard definition; if I cite one or two famous cases of it you will know what I mean. For example, John Bunyan, author of *The Pilgrim's Progress*. One day a voice came darting in his ear to tell him that he could not have both his fun and his salvation. "Wilt thou leave thy sins and go to heaven," it asked, "or have thy sins and go to hell?" He often heard supernatural sayings after that, the poor hysterical man of genius; he made a habit of it, and in his second-best book, *Grace Abounding to the Chief of Sinners*, wrote all about it.

Pascal, the great French mathematician and theologian, was in a carriage crossing a bridge; the horses reared over the parapet, but for a wonder the carriage with him in it stopped on the brink; and ever afterward he had an illusion of a precipice of death and an abyss of eternity gaping at his feet wherever he went, and therefore grew more and more religious, which kept him from going mad. Now I am no such man as that. My experience was not very exalted and not at all tragic. Only psychologically speaking, in its small way, it was of the same character and classification as those famous examples. I do not mean to be pretentious about them; or if I pretend a little, it is only to tell my story more clearly.

I was walking down Madison Avenue, below Fifty-ninth Street on the west sidewalk. I can recall the exact spot: just south of the haberdashery of John Gordon where I buy bargain shirts, just north of the deluxe newsstand of the suave Gottfried brothers where I buy English periodicals. I was about to go into Gottfrieds' to see if they had received any recent issues of *Horizon* and the *New Statesman and Nation*. I was in one of those moods as recurrent as malaria in New Yorkers, when the longing to go abroad makes us ache and sweat. We long to go abroad even when we are most enthusiastic about New York; and anyway, as I have said, I was all out of enthusiasm.

The day before, a widowed friend of mine had consulted me about the education of her fine small boy, and I had looked into two or three of our public schools, and there were half again as many school children as they had room for, crowded in shadowy and evil-smelling rooms like little livestock in a stockyard, and the teachers that I saw were unhappy half-educated political appointees, left over from some period of municipal mismanagement. The night before, someone had taken me to the opera, and our opera is a poor obsolescent institution. That morning, I had visited our museum of old art, which is a melancholy pretentious place; a collection of quantity rather than quality, arranged more or less in the way of a great auction room. If I were a musician or a painter perhaps I should think these time-honored establishments better than nothing. Nothing at all is done for literature. I had spent the luncheon hour and an hour or two after luncheon pleading with an influential friend for the endowment of a new literary magazine; pleading with insufficient eloquence or insufficient patience, at any rate in vain.

The more I thought of all these things, as I came away from my friend's apartment down the street, the worse I felt about them. New York, I said to myself, is a futile and disillusioning and boring place.

Then it happened. Suddenly a voice said to me, or said in me, softly but sternly, "It's all there is, there isn't any more." It was a familiar, noble, husky, not exactly sober tone of voice, with a manner of fanatical fondness pulsing in it, and as a matter of fact I knew at once what long ago memory of mine it derived from. It was Miss Barrymore's voice, when she was young and I was very young, and for a season or two I was infatuated with her; Miss Barrymore's voice in a play by Zoë Akins; a deathbed speech, the dissolute lady of title whom she was portraying having been run over by a taxicab. New York is all there is, the voice admonished, there isn't any more.

That sound recollected from my boyhood, and the meaning of the banal words—in the context of what I had in mind, in connection with the way life went on there in New York in my middle age—moved me and dismayed me. The damp, dulling, shrinking afternoon light, late afternoon in late December, suddenly turned to vision, and the sidewalk was a world and the gutter was an abyss. For a minute I stood there giddy, weak in the knees and short of breath.

For it is a fact that New York is the only city on earth today that is not out of luck, not in a state of siege, not in the clutch of evil invaders, not in tragic travail and shortage and exhaustion fighting for its life! The only very great metropolis left in a position to have everything that you expect of a great metropolis, unless it is Rio de Janeiro which I do not know . . . We have talent enough, money enough, liberty enough. No other city has; it is up to us.

We cannot look to the cities of Europe for our civilization any longer. London will have to be rebuilt before anything else can be expected of it; and Paris and Rome are in the hands of the infidel, the crusade to retake them has just begun. And mere retaking will not really solve their problems. There will be little peace of mind for them in their peace, no luxury or power, for years to come. So now it is our turn. In good fortune, in opportunity, in responsibility, we are unique, which is a frightening thing to be.

There I stood in Madison Avenue. I forgot about *Horizon* and the *New Statesman and Nation*. I remember staring at the newspapers on Gottfrieds' stand beside the door, unable to concentrate on what the headlines said. Then I went on down the street, walking (as the saying is) on air, like a sleepwalker, not bumping into anyone but not seeing anyone either, and when I came to a street corner, crossing without reference to the stop lights. I vaguely remember a traffic policeman's shouting at me at one point. I was so absorbed in my vision of New York—with the rival cities of Europe all out of the running for the time being, disabled by history—that New York itself in fact might have been a thousand miles away. I met two of my friends but I did not notice them, I cut them; they complained of it next day.

I wandered on past one of my favorite shops, namely, the Allerton Fruit Shop: a room which is the size of a good clothes closet packed neatly from top to bottom with rarities to eat, such as saffron and poppy seed, Astrakhan caviar, rum truffles made by refugees, Oriental licorice, et cetera. There is just room enough in the midst of the foodstuffs for the shopkeeper to bow as he tells you that in spite of the war he has whatever you have asked for, and to make change. He is a courteous, reticent, pale man, with a love of the programs of WQXR, especially string quartets. As I reached his door it opened and let out a few bars of Beethoven's opus 131, which added something to my afternoon's emotion. New York is a lovable city.

I loitered around the corner and turned south again on Fifth Avenue. Some errand somewhere along there needed doing, but by the time I reached the place I had forgotten what it was; and I got almost to Thirty-fourth Street, now thinking hard, now walking thoughtlessly, before it occurred to me that I should be late for dinner if I did not turn back toward my own address.

On the far side of Fifth Avenue I saw a little crowd in front of Kress's great cheap store, and over their heads, through the plate glass, amid the usual countless items of merchandise, I could half make out a large color reproduction of a work of art. In the idlest curiosity I crossed over to see what it was. It was not a color reproduction but, as attested by a label alongside it, the world-famous original, "The Adoration of the Shepherds," by Giorgione: elegant shepherds and pearl-faced Virgin and mystic passive stepfather, and the baby Redeemer like a naked lamb on the ground in a pale gray glow. It had been one of the chief masterpieces in the private collection of the proprietor of the store, and he had lately made a gift of it to the nation, as the label also attested. Characteristic of our good cultivated old merchant princes, I thought: with the one hand using culture as a lure to get the crowd in and take their pennies, and with the other hand giving them back a million dollars' worth of old art.

I paused in front of another shop with, not a crowd, only two or three young women, who did not seem amused by it as I was. It was a small place which specialized in attire for women, under-attire, corsetry, and such; and it too had made an effort in its window for the Christmas season. There was a holy family in the pretty commercialized style of Munich, and an ox and an ass, and the three wise men, all in tinted plaster and gimcrack and cellophane. The shepherds had been left out, which, I suppose in the strict order of the festivals of the church, made it Epiphany rather than Christmas. All the upper part and the back of the window were decorated in the semblance of a glorious sky, bright blue, and astronomy of gold foil; and there flew the funniest host of angels you ever heard of, consisting of a selection of the shop's deluxe corsets outfitted with paper wings and suspended in aerial attitudes by means of threads attached to the Lastex and plastic garters and the rayon shoulder straps. The two or three young women, who were pretty, gazed at the upper-left angel with some solemnity, but whether they were considering it as an angel or as something they might be well-advised to buy for their own use I could not tell. Say what you will of Paris, London, Rome, they do not provide for a sense of humor as generously as our town.

When I was a small boy, hearing my pioneer grandparents tell of their early trips west, I confused them with the three wise men, the Three Kings of the Orient. And later I had a little repeating dream in which those three appeared, not wise and royal but young and foolish, wearing coonskin caps and poke bonnets, traveling after their star to Bethlehem by covered wagon and canal boat. Now it seems to me that this childish mistake and infantile dream were not altogether stupid; the Magi in fact must have been like that. They went by their optimism and prognostication, not really knowing what they would find at the spot marked for them on their map of starlight, or what would result from it. They would make very suitable patron saints for us too, now, here on the frontiers of culture and commerce in New York.

Then I turned back uptown, with my grandiose notion of New York, the threat of its failure and the wonder of its future, still in my mind. And I decided that, with no more than my usual pretentiousness—all imaginative men are pretentious, at least all imaginative American men—I could call it a kind of epiphany. The matters of fact and my make-believe were so mixed in it, and seemed so nearly the same thing, that I would never try to distinguish them; and I had so great a sense of its importance and so strange a feeling of my own unimportance that it made me shiver. As plain as day, and as promising, it shone there, as it were, before my eyes, under my nose, in the poor damp dirty street which indeed was no better than a stable, amid the asininity and the bovine simplicity and sloth of my various fellow men pushing along on the sidewalk with me, on their way home to their dinners.

Shop windows, a thousand shop windows, a weary dirty crowd, and things like that, are the factual detail of New York, and I cannot pretend to think any of that beautiful, or important. There was nothing in the shop windows made to last, nothing except Mr. Kress's Giorgione. New York is lovable, strange, and sometimes funny; it is not beautiful or important, yet. It is a thousand things, unfinished, misused, potential, wasted; and until we have great art, especially a great literary art, no one will be able to make much sense of it. It is a question mark, to which imagination keeps answering. No matter whether my particular answer is the right answer; there is an answer, and someone more important than I will find it out before long. It is a promise broken again and again and again, it is vacuous and virgin. I can find fault with it by the hour; and therefore I love it, in view of the fact that it has time and energy enough to remedy everything. I love it because this is its time. I love it because it is lucky. I love it because, like most New Yorkers, I am an optimist.

Oh, it may turn out badly, growing dramatic and tragic as the years go by, in the long run, like the cities of Europe. For God is not mocked, even by American cheerfulness, God is tragic. In any event it will not be the same drama, the old fatalistic theme and trap-like plot. Insofar as we can see ahead in history, we shall not be overthrown by fate, in a kind of mockery of Greek tragedy, as it has been in Europe; nor will it be a mimicry of Wagner, as European historians and philosophers have expressed their sense of fate lately, with an excuse and an alibi for everyone and no hope for anyone. There is plenty of hope for us. If New York fails it will be like a strong young person, in pride and folly, with its future in its power, its heart's desire in its hands, letting it drop. There will be no excuse for us. Perhaps because I am a New Yorker, I prefer that. I think that in the whole of history there has never been a city which had so great a degree of free will.

As I walked back up Fifth Avenue the weather began to change, rapidly and romantically as it does here. The temperature fell, the humidity decreased, the dimness cleared up. With unexpected motion the sky was putting itself in order, the clouds, as the daylight waned out of them, shifting away; then down the west-side side streets a very slight sunset waved like a handkerchief. At the street corners there were little winds; the cold was coming for Christmas. There is a certain hardship in this brilliant, ever vacillating climate, which New Yorkers like. If you relax in it, you collapse, but if you keep from collapsing long enough, you become a part of it and begin to draw upon a certain force by which it seems inhabited. You cease to be tired and you begin to tire others. New York is a hard place to accomplish anything in. Something about it tends to prevent any kind of facility. If you try to do facile work in it, you find yourself doing bad work, which is not the same thing.

It got dark fast; a transparent or translucent darkness. The lights came on. In apartment buildings curtains were drawn, but in office buildings the windows of a million white-collar workers shone, some with long piercing beams, some with a fiery and puffy illumination for them to finish their day's work by. In one skyscraper, idler, darker than the others, a single bulb of who knows how many watts twinkled so strongly that I could not look straight at it. A hotel on the east side looked like a Christmas tree, festooned; but in general the bright scene in the air did not have a holiday aspect; it was solemn. There was nothing crimson or green anywhere except the stop lights up the avenue.

I was pleased, pleased to the point of ecstasy, with everything, everything except the war. And with imagination at work, or at play—I could not tell which—I saw New York in its entirety and immensity in my mind's eye as clearly as Fifth Avenue ahead of me: New York, looming as it does when you come in from flat Long Island, New York as a vast cloud in the river, over the diamond wavelets and ferryboats like glowworms and sad extinguished freighters and fighting ships. And my mind also went to the other extreme: I saw myself there in the street very small, with objectivity and subjectivity mixed in a dream, unreal but not untrue; someone going out to dine presently with his dear one, someone not first-rate and yet all right. A man of promise, ineffectual but resolute, more resolute than before taking this walk.

An Example of Suicide

That midsummer day, when I went down on the Fifth Avenue bus to lunch with a friend, there was a jam of traffic, and the sidewalks for several blocks in the Fifties were crowded. It was not a strike, not a parade, not a motor-accident. Everyone was looking up at the Hotel Gotham, or perhaps the church on the opposite corner. I myself could not discover a thing, which vexed and amused me.

We lunched in Fifty-fifth Street, and when we came out of the restaurant there were upward-gazing people all the way to Madison Avenue. It might have been the homecoming of a flier or something of that sort. The many tilted necks and shaded eyes were very impressive; I thought, with no ribaldry, that it might have been the second coming of the Messiah. By that time the assembly in Fifth Avenue had ominously increased. We made our way into it, and learned what the trouble was: a young man with evidently suicidal intent stood on a very narrow cornice outside the seventeenth floor of the Gotham. He had been there several hours. It was impossible to catch hold of him, and so far, it had been impossible to persuade him to come back inside the building, back away from his death.

The crowd too was in a fantastic state of mind, or of two or three minds: hoping to see him saved; hoping to see him leap, if in fact it could not be prevented; hoping, and also fearing, that it was only a stunt. Especially women here and there were getting into arguments as to what he meant, and whether he "really" meant it, and whether he had a right to trouble his fellow citizens so; and those who thought him a coward or only a publicity-seeker were vehemently, but too vehemently, scornful of the others. In many faces appeared a somewhat affected good cheer; and one or two of both sexes were in an enthusiasm verging upon tearfulness. But for most of them apparently it was a moment not of emotion but of a kind of harassed intellectual effort. They were New Yorkers, that is to say, proud of always understanding what goes on in New York. They were trying to concentrate, in response to, and in spite of each other's innumerable bothering presence; to decide what was happening, what was going to happen, in a hurry, before it happened.

The policemen were having terrible work with them and with the traffic, but they did not curse or blow their whistles loudly; and their faces showed only the kindliest exasperation and anxiety. Some people had equipped themselves with field-glasses. One stout gentleman with a rosy hard old baby-face such as I shall have myself in twenty years, peered up through tiny mother-of-pearl opera glasses. Judging by the solemnity of his squint and the liveliness of his old lips, the close-up of the wretched young man's face must have been wonderful. It was ideal weather, not warm enough to make one hate one's fellow men; and the sun was within a veil, so that it was not blinking. A hurdy-gurdy purveyed its vulgar song down the side-street where the multitude did not prevent it.

At the various vantage-points magnificent newsreel cameras were set up, artillery of our quiet hemisphere; and the cameramen kept their hands on the crank in case he suddenly jumped. So why wait? I asked myself. One would be able to see it, indeed one could scarcely avoid seeing it, at every movie theater in town. The block of West Fifty-fifth Street beneath his perch was closed; and there a good many more policemen and reporters stood around on foot. An ambulance was in readiness. A hook-and-ladder truck came, with restrained clang. But I heard someone say that there was no point in spreading a life-net; he was too high; the strands of a net would cut him all up. Someone else had seen him accept a glass of water from one of the men and women who were leaning out of the hotel window, so near him, yet so far. Someone had heard someone say that those were his mother and brother and sister. I took a good look at him. He was young, slight, handsome. He wore a white shirt and no coat. He was smoking a cigarette, and moved restlessly; and to every move the crowd responded with its immense and confused, if not altogether stupid, sympathy.

I did not wish to see him leap. It was not the waiting with the crowd that I dreaded: the fatigue of waiting, the crowd-sickness. He looked so restless and fatigued that it seemed to me that I should not have to wait long. I was half ashamed of my disinclination. Is it not part of my literary business to see things, and have I not always enjoyed that part at least? Certainly there would be details of which my imagination would not be apt to inform me, which the candidest photographer could not catch, and which, I dare say, only a Hemingway or a Porter could describe more nicely than I: the heave and the gulp of the crowd when it happened; the tint of the overcast heaven just then; the white-shirted shape just how darkened, just how deformed, by its velocity downward. . . . No matter; I would not stay. It was from my own melancholy, not the young man's, that I fled; and it was hard work, slow going, through the upset populace. Now, alas, having started the writing of this little commentary, I must reconsider and be instructed by my own case, which is unpleasant and perhaps unwholesome.

❧

Waiting at home all that summer afternoon to hear what finally happened, I believed—and I still believe—that in the worst way in the world the young man wanted to quit it, give up, go back inside the hotel room. I looked at him strictly, and I am fairly perceptive. Surely it was not the hard or fond face of the true idealizer of death, or the man who has deliberated and found death the lesser of two evils. It was an afraid face, afraid of altitude and abyss and hard pavement among other things. But, oh, what a difficult and disgraceful predicament he was in! Right there behind him was the window full of his intimates passionately watching him, mother and brother and sister perhaps, persons who all the rest of his life might be expected to complain of him, to patronize him, to make fun of him and trip him up—if he let them conclude that when he slipped out on the ledge in the first place he had no serious intention of suicide. That intention was his trump-card, and he had shown it, only hesitated to play it. What if he had changed his mind? How could he explain that change to them, so as to prevent their condemnation and entire disrespect? What would life with them be like if he did not kill himself? The present set-up had come to this. From this point on he would have to play some new game; at least he would have to get away from the present players. How could he? All day long he kept politely requesting his would-be rescuers to let him alone, to let him think.

I am no psychiatrist; yet I dare say that if I had been in charge I should have sent someone he had never seen before into that hotel room to put a five-hundred or a thousand dollar bill on the table by the window where he could see it, and to call out to him that it was his if he wanted it, but that he might do as he liked, jump if he liked. Also I should have lectured his family severely and encouragingly, and given them some potent sedative, and sent them home. Then I should have asked the police department to arrange a detour for the Fifth Avenue traffic, and to oblige the crowd also to go about its business, so that no one should see what he did. Perhaps after dark he might have slipped inside and taken the money and gone somewhere: an evasion of the issue, a postponement. Yes, I know: in a few months he might have been found out on another limb, another ledge. But what more can any man do than postpone his death? As it was, all New York was horribly saying, Now or never! Ah, yes, it meant well.

What pain of fumbling treatment, and bitterness of mistaken medicine! Not to mention the damage done irreparably the instant this all started. For even if he gave up and let himself be saved and never attempted it again, his psyche would be much the worse for wear, I thought. Hours of this shilly-shally, how habit-forming!— poised between the world and the devil, with the thousand world-lings at his feet, their imaginations somewhat at the mercy of his, a thousand little shapes of no more consequence to him than his own shadow. . . . Surely it was enough to swell and turn a man's head forever, and in more ways than one. Part of his character must have slipped over the edge, Humpty-Dumpty, whatever the rest of body and soul decided.

What interested me and indeed closely concerned me was not the outcome of his hesitation—life or death, life with a deformation, or death by tumbling and smashing—but the nature of it. Not the present occasion and the immediate provocation, but the trouble that he must have had with himself almost every day for years, similar to this trouble, inconspicuously bringing him little by little to this point. Not the individual instance, but the general modern habit of mind, plight of mind: the combination of a doleful and illusory lone-liness with a sudden embarrassing sense of humanity as a whole, which more and more arises and afflicts most of us. My own habit and plight. . . . This young man's showy death served me and suited me as an instructive example and allegory.

For the formula of almost all our lives now is this: individual excitement is prized more highly than anything, yet is shame-faced finally; and the collectivity is regarded as rather remote and beneath contempt, yet is most fascinating, casts the final spell. We mean to act individualistically, selfishly, but we cannot keep it up. In the time of crisis we lose interest in ourselves. We suddenly see ourselves as playing a part before an audience, which confuses us. It is hard to think what we ought to do; it is too hard; it is impossible. We can no longer do just what we feel like doing; so fascinated are we by what we think that others are thinking. Of two minds— mind inactive, introspective, and mind as it were stage-struck and stage-frightened—very often at last our action is accidental. We intend to leap; at least that is our hypothesis or threat. Suddenly we change our minds, but it is too late. Therefore we *fall*.

Now in fact I myself have never stood vacillating like this fellow, hour after hour without a will, between life and death. My youthful threats of an attempt at suicide were only hysteria, easy to thwart, and not habit-forming. I believe that the state of this young man's mind must not have been hysteria, but only a kind of extreme inability to think of himself, for himself: a daze, a weariness, a paralysis, a daydream. Possibly hysterical self-indulgence caused it, in the way that other excesses result at last in other impotencies. Or perhaps disgraceful behavior served as a kind of stimulant or counter-irritant to prevent, that is, to postpone it. Both might be true. In any case, the care and cure and handling of it by the family and psychiatrists and upon occasion the police and even acquaintances and bystanders—especially the control of it as innocently, dreamily, gradually, it comes about in one's self—must fail unless it is understood to be different from hysteria. "Scenes," delusion and unreasonableness and evil temper are activities. It is in a passive state, unselfishly, perhaps virtuously, that one dies.

Obviously this is an unscientific distinction, loose opinion. I can vouch for it only in the vain way of the poet or novelist or dramatist—by avowal of psychic adventure and infirmity of my own. Little inward suicide of my own, a bit at a time, the while I have gone on rather enviably and not undignifiedly living . . . Not madness at all, but only careless ways of thinking and feeling and talking by which I have driven myself and others almost "mad." Not evil, but gradual, mechanical forfeitures of the opinion of those whose enthusiasm about me I most require. Not vice, but various debauch and despoiling of my talent: literary imagination let go in a sort of onanism, revery, riddle; the will to write depressed and dismembered; book after book aborted, and so forth. All of this perfectly undramatic, all harmless, and all petty, not worth committing suicide about— yet, I dare say relevant. For little by little it might have brought me to a point of modesty and mediocrity at which it would have been a good idea to kill myself, the thing to do next, the suitable dramatic gesture. I suppose it may still. In any case it seems that my type of unhappiness and unsuccessfulness is to be thought of with reference to the jumper's type of suicide, and vice versa. The one is metaphorical of the other. Also, certain inferences may be made from this, as to the general course of modern morality, the will of millions, the fate of nations. . . .

When I was a child someone taught us to hypnotize a hen. We drew a chalk line on a porch floor or a sidewalk, and put her down, outstretched on it: her claws close together, her bill pointed along it, and her small stupid, semi-precious eyes looking down her bill. Then, softly, we took our hands off her. She lay there a long time— until something happened to move somewhere within her line of vision, and distracted her.

It is in the inaction, not the action, that the subtlest danger lies; and in the maze of good intentions rather than in evil impulse; and in excesses of patience and passivity rather than in hysterics. What though it be amid an overt brawling aggressive trouble or misbehavior that—like the still small voice of the god Jehovah in the midst of storm—the mind first hears its murmuring to itself. Then it may be late, perhaps too late; for some still small troublesome idea, mere petty detail, is the god, the working of whose will the trouble is. Usually we are deaf to ourselves, deaf as posts. And early every morning we start rocking ourselves to sleep lest we do something unreasonable, disgraceful during the day. We bankrupt ourselves day by day, by behaving in minor matters better than we can afford. Or we go on dreaming of behaving well until, when we must awake, we are exhausted; accident and shame suddenly take charge of us; self-consciousness is all we know; and what it is possible of us to do has ceased to seem a reality to us, has become a drama.

I think that even the outrageous end of a man like the one at the hotel, even clownishly clambering out on a skyscraper-ledge over New York, is essentially only an effort to wake up, to snap out of it. He needed to frighten himself a little; he frightened others as well, and thrilled them, and angered them; and he stayed spellbound by this all day long. The term "flight from reality"—which is, roughly speaking, the key to current psychiatry, and must be ordinarily applicable and useful—is misleading in such a case. Having fled from reality again and again, perhaps habitually, suddenly such a man comes face to face with some little bit of it; and it startles him out of his wits, immobilizes him, hypnotizes him. Once this dumbfounding, this nonplussing, has taken place, it is the real, not the unreal, that is dangerous. A suitable lie or a sentimental reminder or a symbolic gesture, a gift of money, a new acquaintance, a night in a brothel, might have saved him. His relatives, loving or otherwise, and the horde of New Yorkers waiting to learn who he really was, what he really wanted, what he would actually do at last, and the might of the municipality in its great stupid good will aroused by him and outwitted by him—that must have been too real to be borne.

For the real at a given instant may well be on the side of death. In reality, a good deal of the time, there are a good many things that cannot be helped. Upon occasion there may be quite good enough reasons to kill oneself or to do various other violence. They need not be great or romantic or dramatic reasons. Poor wretches like this one happen to see them suddenly, expire of amazement, stumble to death. Obviously they should have been wearing intellectual eyeglasses of suitable focus for some time; modern education as a rule fails to provide any. In the hour of their emergency, the hour of blinding light, nothing will do except a blindfold. Apparently no one at his seventeenth-story deathbed thought of that.

How rare it is after all for a man to come to his bad end conspicuously! But there are a great number of us who, perfectly familiar with sufficient reasons to kill ourselves, will not. Nor will we allow ourselves to have hysterics every time we feel like it; nor do harm willingly; nor go raving mad even temporarily, if we can help it.

Think of what is well known now about the suffering of the psyche, and how it adjusts itself or fails to adjust itself. Neglect of some childish sensuality, or a supposed triumph over an essential temptation, or it may be fear, or shame, or refusal to remember whatever has been most shockingly shameful, causes the kind of distress and failure that is customarily called neurosis. (Balzac and Dostoevsky each called it something else.) Well, for some people, for me, and perhaps you, and you, refusal to indulge oneself in this primary distress, refusal to lie and quarrel and have hysterics, refusal to die, refusal to kill, may bring about another bad psychic condition, "neurosis" of another sort. To behave well, with respect to this or that mishap, in this or that lifelong predicament, may weaken you and disgrace you on the whole. The best things in life in the long run probably cost less than the worst; they are not free. The wages of virtue must be paid, as well as those of sin. Humanity has all at last to be accounted in the same currency. Suppose you give in about something, as you must or as you should; you renounce a particular desire or hope. Alas, you may find yourself in consequence of this, "relaxed" in every other way as well. A peculiar languor, a seemingly strong hesitation, may result simply from forgiveness. Desperate lethargy may be a substitute for hysterics. Suicide may be, or at least seem, the only alternative to murder. The more complex the type of person you are, the more painful and mysterious your problem. . . . Even great love as the years pass generates a certain vengefulness. See how the lovers with might and main, in order that love shall last, strive to prevent this or some other venomous byproduct of love from taking effect. But the striving, the strife, cannot be prevented. How disgraceful; what a waste of time and energy! Yet, if they are too proud to fight quietly, secretly, as long as they live, they are more than likely to come to the divorce court.

So it goes, this way, that way, up and down the scale of human purpose, up and down the price range of morality. The poor young man's position from start to finish must have been fairly far down. Probably his life could have served no purpose at all if it had not happened by its finale to entertain and inspire and appall thousands of New Yorkers all one afternoon.

About six o'clock when the friend with whom I live came home, he reported that the terrible youth was still perched. The crowd had distinguished somewhat: dinnertime. The spirit of the thing, I gathered, had settled to a sadder, more boring, perhaps morbid level.

My friend, a lordly kind of man, impetuous, with a sharp simplicity of speech, expressed mingled scorn and skepticism and indignation. "What nonsense!" he said. "This man is nothing but a fool, or else a fraud, or else a lunatic. The traffic policemen are the ones to be pitied. And the passion of the mob, how silly, sinister! Surely they could lasso the poor wretch, or something, if they tried hard, if they wanted to. Anyway, surely, finally, he'll give up and come in. America will give him its hero worship for a few days. He'll be able to make personal appearances in movie theaters for a few weeks. . . ." I was sorry that I could not share my friend's optimism; and his sensitive cynicism displeased me.

My evening paper reported that a slight quarrel with the two sisters who were at the Gotham with the man had provoked his terrible resolution, irresolution. So those were the women I had seen leaning out of the window, pleading with him. One reporter heard one of them call out to him, "All right, John. I admit that you have more character than I have." So that was what it was all about. It did not surprise me. Lack of character is one of the classic themes of fatal argument. So now it was up to little brother to prove that he had at least enough character to die. If he could overcome his evident repugnance to death, he would prove it, and in spectacular fashion. Hour after hour of repugnance and burden of proof! Manifesto: the secret of most suicides; the strange mania of the entire human species when hurt, and, let us not forget, the basis of the new disastrous aspect of world politics, the new diplomacy. . . . I wished the young man well, and suddenly and strangely realized at this point that, practically speaking, it amounted to wishing him dead.

I was reminded of an anecdote of the childhood of Louis XV, King of France. Old Cardinal Fleury, his tutor, scornfully remarked that indeed he could not be expected to act against his own affection or inclination, because, alas, he lacked will-power. What a poor prospect for his kingdom! At the time there was only one thing in the world for which the child-king felt any affection: a little pet deer. So he ordered that brought to him, and shot it. Perhaps tears dimmed his eyes, or his hand shook; he only wounded it with his first shot but he resolutely took aim again. I have always thought that this may have had something to do with his indifference and insensibility throughout his life, alas for France. His heart may have been all scar-tissue.

I was also reminded of the death of Bramwell Bronte. In that family of burning sentiment and iron resolve Bramwell was the characterless one; a creature of procrastination and prevarication, of vice and whim, good for nothing. His relatives despaired of him, pitied him. When he fell ill he announced that it was his intention to die standing up. He might not have another chance to prove himself as resolute as the rest of us. And, while the terrible sisters knelt around, weeping, praying, he did manage to stay on his feet until his heart stopped, until his corpse fell.

On the midsummer night of the trial of our New York Bronte's character, several friends of ours attended the dancing on the Mall in Central Park and paid us a call after that, about midnight. They brought the news that—because he was tired out, because he had drunk water that his sisters handed out to him all afternoon, or, perhaps, because by that time he really had considered everything and come to a conclusion—he had fallen from his high place. Down from the seventeenth-story ledge like a falling star in a quick whitish streak he had slipped, or, possibly, leapt. Down into West Fifty-fifth Street, paved, like hell, with good intentions. Mincemeat on the doorstep of the deluxe hotel. . . .

By that time, we were told, there were three hundred policemen on duty, and ten thousand spectators. Only by courtesy indeed could many of them be called spectators. They were herded together away down the avenue and in the side-street, far from the terrible view, the fatal pavement. Those who could not see must have come, that is, must have stayed, simply for the pleasure of herding; the improvised friendships, anonymous affections; the long irresponsible caresses from head to foot as they pushed or fidgeted or bided the time; the multitudinous body-odor, like cypress and like ambergris; the intense wrath of conjoined soul as well as assembled body. And no doubt they admired the three hundred uniforms, the radio-cars and ambulance, the thousand-dollar cameras, the splendid cheerful floodlights: ideal modernity of which New Yorkers hear so much and see so little. Even the very short ones and young ones down under the elbows and amid the warm hearts and upset stomachs of the tall majority, heard the strange collective choral groan with which the poor man was saluted at last. Even the heartless, the unimaginative, must have experienced to some extent, by vibration, contagion, the gooseflesh of their fellowmen. Most of them, I think, by remembrance of and comparison with weak moments of their own in the past, must have understood almost all that was going on in the wretched hero's mind as he nodded and swayed, high and mighty in his way there in the electrified night. I suppose they were too humble and too uncultured to try to do that.

The morning of course brought morning papers, with a great deal of amplification and correction as usual, and here and there a resourceful or spiteful note; for even reporters suffer from a kind of moral hangover. Then the various picture-publications appeared: snapshots of the flight to earth of the young pleasureless body from every angle, wonderfully snapped, out of focus, with a swishing dim tail like that of a comet. Finally the news-weeklies summarized it all in their way, concise and supercilious, too wily to give opinions, but with plenty of snap-judgments slipped into the ostensibly pure narration to speed it up. And by this time almost everyone will have forgotten almost all about it.

The young man had only one sister in fact. The others whom I had seen leaning out of the window were an older married couple, close friends. Evidently he was madder than he looked; this was not his first suicidal attempt, and he spent last year in a madhouse. But surely it was a gentle derangement, melancholic, innocuous, for the friendly couple, to help him get hold of himself, had not hesitated to engage him as their children's tutor. Therefore I dare say that there is no great distortion of truth in my thought of him as interestingly representative of a type of ordinary and nervous man, the man who is proud as Lucifer yet ashamed of and put to shame by himself.

I must have been right in supposing that he regretted his rash act before he could complete it. A reporter heard him tell his sister that he would be "ashamed" and "embarrassed" to give up and not jump—having assembled in honor of his mixed motives this superb mournful, scornful multitude, well-wishers and skeptics and sensation seekers and what not.

When I said to myself that it would be a good idea to try tempting him with a five-hundred dollar bill, bribing him to live a while longer, I wondered where the money would come from. But it has been estimated that his sensational death as it happened cost the city of New York one hundred thousand dollars.

In case this meditation of mine should be printed, let me address a deferential word to such a man's relatives and friends. I do not pretend that all this is true, much less the whole truth. I followed the newspapers, and doubtless forget a part of what I read, and perhaps then remembered more than was written. For my modest purpose it sufficed to be approximative. I did not even verify my anecdotes about the King of France and the Bronte brother. How can I be sure of my judgment even of my own psyche? And why should I be sure? It is all supposition, a kind of fiction, and an example of the preventive misdemeanor that I recommend, for the psyche's sake—to prevent my ever doing what he did.

I think of another instance of dangerous American clowning which is not aristocratic at all, but only a sort of allegory. When the young man stood out on the seventeenth-story ledge of the Gotham threatening to throw himself down, his friend said, "Come on, John, come back in and we'll go to a baseball game." John had always been a fan, and the Giants were playing that afternoon.

"Who are they playing?" he inquired, and his friend felt hopeful. "The Dodgers." It is a notoriously bad team.

"I'd rather die than see the Dodgers," the wretched creature exclaimed; and once more his attention turned to the frightful game he was playing himself. Indeed it would be silly to say that he died to prove how much he despised the Dodgers. But almost certainly he died to prove something; and it may have been only a figure of speech in the first place.

The Odor of Rosemary

In 1935 I found myself aboard a middle-sized, very comfortable, new Italian liner named the *Conte di Savoia*, voyaging toward the Strait of Gibraltar along the south coast of Spain; and there, surprisingly, a great odor of rosemary descended from the Iberian mountain slopes to meet us, out of sight of land. It seemed the very soul and ghost of divine Earth; and it fixed itself in my mind as a metaphor for the good fortune of my existence overall and of the existence of the entire human species, relatively speaking. More fortunate, more blissful, than any other animal's existence!

I was traveling with my brother and his wife, recently married and going abroad together for the first time. In the morning and most of the afternoon I kept out of their way, and with time on my hands, consequently, I made friends with two or three fellow passengers, among them a very odd youngster, whose name has slipped my mind. I have, however, kept in my remembrance word for word (it seems) an autobiographical story that he told me, and a few stray amusing or pleasing remarks.

What was odd about him? Oddity in reverse. He had not (I thought) a single trait or peculiarity that would help me to remember him, if for any reason I should want to. He was simply everyman at an early age; John Doe Jr. I did not find him handsome, recognizing nevertheless that he had certain fine features: a clear complexion and blushing cheeks and good teeth; and soft, almost dim hazel eyes that gleamed a little, once in a while. Though slim he was obviously strong, but he moved in an unenergetic way and he was rather awkward. His hair was yellow and unbecomingly cut, and I thought his suits and ties vulgar. His manners, on the other hand, were gentle and unassuming. His expression brightened pleasantly when I talked to him, but very evidently he had an indolent mind and a minimum of education.

Even familiar friends, if they had seen him and me together, might have assumed that I was attracted to him physically. I was not. What other compatibility could there have been between us? Ego, to start with, another measure of the interest of all things, and of one's fellowmen. My first thought about him was that he must have been approximately the age that I was in 1921, voyaging with such mixed emotions, minding the lack of modern improvements, dismayed by the seasick November weather, some fifteen latitudinal degrees farther north. A kind of sentimental interest: what did this voyage mean to him?

Another of my vulnerabilities in those years, quite distinct from ego and libido, was curiosity; greatly abated now. It appertained to my young vanity and optimism as a writer; also abated or at least changed. I used to pray for subject matter, to watch for it and track it down and lure it out of people and make it mine. Now my prayer is: no more of that, no more; not another hint or another glimpse, beyond what I can handle; nothing unsuited to my talent. Any new thing to write about, suitable or not, gives me a bad conscience, as it will crowd out something that I already have in mind, in hand. Enough is as good as a feast, better than a feast.

The young man who perhaps suggested subject matter to me, despite his ordinary aspect, sat at our table. Beginning on the second or third day, we took our exercise together, round and round the deck. Sometimes in the evening he would sit in the bar with me and my brother, and with my sister-in-law also, once or twice, when the sea was calm and the vessel steady. He was not particularly drawn to me. His hazy-looking hazel eyes would shift from person to person, as we walked or as we sat, in vain; and then come back to me. There were no youngsters his age, and only a few unattached women and girls, and no good-looking unmarried older men. He was left at loose ends, and we were at ease together.

On the third morning he felt emboldened to ask some questions. "Have you been to Europe before? Where are you going in Italy?"

I answered in some detail, and he in turn told me where he was going. "My friend is at Lido, near Venice. I'm going to meet him there."

That afternoon, or perhaps the next morning, he inquired a little further, as to my place of residence in our native land, my domestic circumstances, and my source of income. "Do you just travel around, living on investments? Are you on vacation? Have you a job or a business?"

I am always less shy about answering questions than about asking them. This time I covered a good deal of ground. Up to that point he hadn't seemed very warmly interested in my account of myself. But when I said, "I'm a writer," he came to life.

"Oh, oh, so you're a writer? A real writer who writes books? Any best sellers?"

No real writer who writes books, especially novels and stories, will be surprised at my saying that this question and answer changed matters between my shipboard acquaintance and me. Around practitioners of literature, meritorious or successful or both or neither, there is a magnetic field, from which some people flee, toward which others gravitate.

The gravitaters as a rule are those who have had extraordinary experiences either in the whole course of life or in some historic juncture or convulsion of chance, or by virtue of a peculiar gift for living or great vulnerability in some way. For example, an octogenarian woman in the Middle West whom I knew as a teenaged boy. In her early teens, she had sat all night with a rifle across her lap, waiting for one last southward thrust of the redskins, out of their desperate reservation in the north woods; which, as it turned out, was a false alarm. For example, a Greek underground hero between wars, or to be exact, between battles, in New York for remedial surgery; a matter of resetting broken bones in his right wrist and right hand, to enable him to press a trigger quicker. For example, a homosexual Italian young man, or perhaps I should say, grown boy, whose father in righteous indignation shot his lover to death, and was acquitted for so doing. I could give example after example; they all wanted, perhaps still want, will always want, to be immortalized. Their aggressiveness in this desire, their indiscretion, and their trustfulness, often amaze us.

My shipboard companion was not aggressive. But, having heard that I was a writer, he felt no further curiosity about me or my life. In certain expressions passing across his face I could see all his thought veering around to himself: his fate, his guilt or innocence, his weakness or strength, in whatever balance, enacted in whatever had happened to him, or might still happen. At last, at last, I sensed that the point of his questioning me was to be questioned back. "Where were you born?" I asked. "Where do you live? Where did you go to school? Did you go in for sports? Do you read a lot? What do your parents do? What are they like?"

Then suddenly he responded with his entire story in a succession of short sentences; in an incongruous tone of voice, soft, ordinary, cold. "Can you believe it? I was born and always lived in a kind of little town named Prison City, California. My parents came from Europe, my father from Sweden, my mother from Italy; but they weren't like foreigners at all. They are both dead. My mother died a little while after my father died. My father killed himself. They were poor people. I was poor too, of course, until just lately. I have a friend who is well-off.

"There used to be a real prison in Prison City. Now it's a reform school for girls; criminal girls, only they're the ones that aren't hard to handle. It's a kind of progressive institution that looks like a campus, with landscape gardening. My father was the gardener and got to be the outdoor superintendent. He had an affair with one of the girls. She was only fifteen years old, but mature for her age; she'd had a baby. For my dad, it was on the up and up; he fell in love with her. My mother knew about it; she hated him anyway. If he hadn't been in love he might have got away with it. He told my mother that there had been a couple of other scandals at the place that had been hushed up. He went to Florida on his vacation with my mother and wrote some love letters from there to the girl. The woman on the staff of the place who had charge of the girls' mail opened the letters he'd written. They weren't just sentimental letters; they were about their making love and all the rest of it. As soon as he got back from Florida they fired him, and they were going to bring him to trial, because the girl was so young. When he heard that, he didn't come home for lunch or dinner; he just killed himself.

"When he didn't come home at all that night, my mother thought he'd gone somewhere and got drunk. The house we lived in had a horse barn behind it. We didn't ever have horses; it was our garage. You could go upstairs over it, which used to be for hay, and we kept things there. I haven't any idea why I went there in the morning. Maybe my mother asked me to bring down a suitcase, or maybe I was looking for an old broken bicycle that I thought I could fix. Afterward I couldn't remember any of that. I opened the door at the foot of the stairs and looked up. There was a beam over the stairs, and my dad's body was hanging there."

He paused, and I couldn't think of anything to say. He looked at me so intently that a good many seconds, perhaps several minutes, seemed to pass. Then he went on. "After it happened, especially after my mother died, I went wild, little by little. It wasn't the body hanging up in the barn. I think you get a kick, when you're a kid, finding something like that. I wasn't close to my dad, and he couldn't have helped me; he was a weak man. I kept thinking that what happened to him wasn't fair; he must have felt that he just had to kill himself. It could happen to anyone; that scared hell out of me.

"I knew this friend in Sacramento and he felt sorry for me, the way I was taking it. We've been together for two years. This year we're going to travel." His golden eyes were as vague and his young voice was as flat when he came to his good fortune as they had been during the narration of his father's romance and self-destruction.

Incorrigible man of letters even then, I said to myself: he hasn't told it well. Oh, this is the great letdown and miscarriage of literature in our time. Most of us tell one another everything, or almost everything; we don't write everything. Society consists of people who, tolerant or intolerant, can be trusted not to repeat what they have heard except to other people who can be trusted. Things written will be read, or at least talked about, by people who can't be trusted; by your children and your aged parents and your poor relations, by your employer and your employees, by your lawmakers and your law-enforcers. What we write is a synthesis and a collage and a composite. Or we write about the lower classes who can't strike back. Very few of us have the courage to write for posthumous publication; it means too great a deprivation of possible income, for one thing. Also, it seems harder work than when a publisher is waiting; and the tape recorder isn't going to help. Spoken narration is too flat, too cold, and not sensuous enough.

Did I think of all this at the time? Did something that I thought transpire in the look on my face, which worried the poor narrator? I have forgotten to say where we were during his narration, which must have taken ten minutes. It was just before dinner; I lay back in my deckchair, and he sat at right angles to me in his adjacent deck-chair. I must have said something; I wonder what, I hope that I didn't suggest to him that I had any superior opinion or explanation of the events he had confided to me, I hope that I didn't sound bored.

Then he said, in a louder voice than he had found for the story itself, "Oh, I'm afraid you haven't liked my blabbing all this to you. My God, let's talk about something cheerful!"

Silence again, and then, to ease him down from that high point of his immature life, and furthermore, to ease myself, I took him into the bar and seated him beside my brother's wife, who, I remember, was inclined to be silent in those early days of her marriage. No matter; even without words, she was good with everyone.

I went a little way across the room and sat at someone else's table. From time to time he glanced across at me, with a look of embarrassment and at the same time of some satisfaction, glad to have the matter off his chest and to have interested me so much.

During the remaining days of our voyage naturally I kept watch for any suggestion or symptom of what his father's transgression and the ugly outcome had done to him. Never for a moment did he seem tragic or even unhappy; just somewhat broken-spirited. Only in semblance was he a boy; in fact he was a man, one who had lost some illusions.

I can recall one other talk with him, which was the day that the mountain breezes or foothill breezes brought the odor of rosemary out to us; down at sea level, amid the salty breathing and trough and crest of divine Ocean. That this sometimes happens I had read in a travel book or a magazine, but supposed that it was a fabrication or a fantasy. We stood in a place on the deck where there was both sunshine and shade. Facing me, the man from Prison City rested his awkward young figure against the port rail, with the light on his coarse yellow hair. I was gazing to the north or the northeast, imagining that I saw dolphins—either that was an optical illusion, or they swam with unnatural rapidity into the distance, with their generic loping movement, like flight without wings—when suddenly the bittersweet smell assailed my nostrils, startling and gratifying.

I called my companion's attention to it. He smiled with all his white teeth and drew several breaths, pleased to show participation in my olfactory experience. "Is it just a foreign plant," he asked, "or is it the same at home? It smells like something, I guess it's something to eat."

I told him that a good many Americans season lamb or veal with it, and that I myself, when I can get it, like to snip a sprig into a tomato salad; better to my taste than basil.

"No kidding!" said he, with his astonished smile and the gleam in his brown-and-yellow eyes.

I might have told him that it grows wild in New Mexico as well as in Andalusia and the Carpathians and other glamorous portions of world-geography. The New Mexicans call it romero weed. The famous Brotherhood of Penitents, or their mothers and their wives, concoct a salve or an embrocation of it, analgesic and disinfectant—or they used to, when I was there as a nineteen-year-old—to treat the lesions up and down their backs due to their ritual flagellation during Holy Week. I believe that I decided to say nothing about that. The Sangre de Cristo Range and the San Juan Mountains seemed too far a cry from the scenes of this poor shocked fellow's past life in Prison City; too far also from his future on the Lido and elsewhere. Also, I always feel some inhibition about the subject matter of sadomasochistic Roman Catholic ritual.

My mind raced back to a thrilling village up in the mountains over the Rio Grande. Above the village a large ravine ascended like a vast flight of stairs, and at the head of it stood a small mountain, a green pyramid suffused with falling snow. Against this background the penitents, naked to the waist, slowly strode along according to their tradition; right foot forward, then a crack of the whip up over the left shoulder, left foot forward, then a crack of the whip over the right shoulder; and soon the blood ran down their backs, down to their loose white underpants. Against the distant snowfall they lit themselves like candles of blood-red wax for the edification of their neighbors in the village, who watched them from a little distance. There was music, played on homemade flutes and sung in sixteenth-century Spanish. I saw one of their whips afterwards: loosely braided fiber with a few bits of tin and glass fastened into the large strands. Calling all this to mind, I took pleasure in the thought of the use of *ros marinus*, the all-purpose plant, for the alleviation of superstitious wounds. Compassion can be a pleasure.

I wonder if I didn't tell my poor friend all this, sleeptalking as others sleepwalk; memory of its own accord and in its own right, sounding off. Certain it is that when I snapped out of my reverie and attended to my interlocutor once more, he gave me a puzzled look.

We went up on the sundeck, and for another quarter of an hour, while still thinking gratefully and with humor of what I was inhaling, recalling not only the differences of opinion about the best uses of rosemary in cooking and salad-making but my various other favorite confusions in folklore about it, bee-food and sting-component and fairyland awakener and energizer—and indeed, letting my fantasy wander as behooved it, far away in space and far back in time, the story of the sweet perspiration of Egyptian heat imbuing the Virgin Mary's cloak and subsequently staining the little pallid flowers of primeval rosemary blue, blue—I carried on further pleasantly desultory conversation with my Californian.

"We'll be sighting land before long," I said. "There is a promontory, called I forget what, that we may see just a shadow of, on the horizon. It's in the lower left corner of the map of Spain."

"Is Spain an island?" the youth on his way from Prison City or from Sacramento to the Lido wanted to know.

"No, no," I answered in an unemphatic voice, in order not to wound him in his self-esteem. He had a quality that would inspire kindness in almost anyone, I thought.

"Oh, I remember now," he said, with something of a child's enthusiasm when it has learned its lesson. "It's Portugal that's the island."

Deep-seated in our poor humanity is covetousness. It is a vacuum and we want it filled. We call upon imagination, no matter how, to counteract our childishness with experience true or false, to beguile our tedium, and to give consolation, when this or that obvious reality has disappointed or frustrated us. Credulity is another immense characteristic; it also helps us with our hearts' desires and the void in our minds. It is contributory to the strength of love and the effectiveness of literature, and enters into other spheres of the spiritual life, some of them unsavory. And I conclude that the sense of smell especially ministers to all this.

Therefore, from time to time, in the years that have elapsed, I have asked myself whether the odor that day, the great whiff of Spain, was imaginary. I have answered myself, No. Why should it be? Either it is true or it is my madness; that is to say, a truth about me.

It would not have occurred to me to invent a breeze-ful of the aroma of a very common herb, and to add interest to it by simply situating it where it was not, had not been, never will be. How can I prove what I say? How can you disprove it? I do not, I could not, ask you to accept the corroboration of my Californian, even if he were at hand and remembered standing there on the *Conte di Savoia* beside me and taking deep breaths. For if I, taking my deep breaths, had declared that I detected, for example, the icy, deadly sweetness of the North Pole—or, for example, the heroic body odor of Alexander the Great in battle (immortalized for us by Plutarch)—that most unheroic boy would have agreed with me. Why? Because I had listened respectfully to his tale.

Read this as fiction if you prefer to. A part of fiction is error, and another part is forgetfulness; and when a great many years have passed, the same is apt to be true of truth. Allow all you like for that; still there will be something that life has implanted in one man's mind, if not in many men's minds, and that life, later on, has called forth in the way of inspiration. It is the details that persuade us of great things. It is the uninventable that we choose to believe and to love in the end. Down from the steep mountainside fields, impossible to cultivate, humming with the wings of bees and sharp with their stings, down came (and down still comes) the musky and honied odor of the herb. Out of the mouth of a commonplace and traumatized boy may issue uninventable words also: his saying at the end of his sorrowful tale, "My God, let's talk about something cheerful!" which touched my heart; and his saying, as his make-believe geography lesson, "Portugal's the island." Yes, let it be the island.

Appendix

Two Essays and
an Experimental Story

The Valley Submerged

Beginning in the mid-thirties my family (including myself) resided in Union Township, Hunterdon County, New Jersey. In 1957 it was decided to expropriate us and to turn our entire valley into a reservoir. The waters of Spruce Run and of Mulhocoway Creek were to be held back in winter and spring, then gradually released in summer, so as to equalize the flow of the Raritan River of which they are tributaries. Now I will tell you what this meant to me at the time, and what lessons I seemed to learn from it, some of which I have had to unlearn.

In point of fact, it was to have been expected. In the late twenties certain real estate speculators, foreseeing the future usefulness of the two streams and a dozen adjacent properties along them, lobbied to have that tract inundated *pro bono publico*. But, as it turned out, another sale in the northern part of the state was selected and submerged instead, which made available the good-sized farm acquired by my brother and sister-in-law some years later, all bottom land. After the war the lower Raritan developed into one of the most flourishing industrial areas in the nation, with vastly increased population and water-requirements which, before long, were going to amount to a continuous emergency. Inevitably the Spruce Run and Mulhocoway project was reconsidered and set in motion once more.

A number of families in the valley banded together to oppose the forced purchase and abolishment of these dear homes and fertile fields, in which opposition my aged mother who had recently come to live with me, and my sister-in-law who was in delicate health, were inclined to join. My brother and I understood that it was hopeless. Furthermore, we were aware of the perilous general lowering of the water table in our part of the world, and, in principle, we believed in the return of a good deal of unnecessary farmland to a condition of wilderness once more: lake, swamp, woodland, and wild acreage. My brother's and sister-in-law's house was to be under forty or fifty feet of water, the state officials told us; mine and my mother's under only ten.

That same summer and early autumn New Jersey suffered a bad drought; irony of the heavens! For the first time in twenty years the brook that encircled my lawn shrank into mere mud. The pastures got in so moribund a condition that the soil loosened under the shrunken grasses, eroded in the breeze. Leaves in the hedgerow withered and hung down around their stems. In some places even burdock and thistle and poison ivy died. So many of the greens having faded out of the landscape, there appeared an odd new color or non-color; and sometimes in the middle of the day, when the sunlight was perpendicular, it seemed to darken, as a dead body may be seen to do: inner flesh casting its shadow through the skin. On and off we felt a kind of passivity, in accord with the general distress of nature, alternating with the characteristic human rebound of excitement and sentiment, dramatization of sadness, unrealistic love of life.

"*Pleurs de joie!* Tears of joy!" Is that not what Pascal had written on a piece of paper folded up or wadded up in a little sack on a string around his neck, referring to his great mystic experience: thunderstruck, lightning-struck sense of doom and simultaneously of salvation, dated November 23, 1654? Nothing of that kind has ever been experienced by me; no real occultism. Presumably I am incapable of it, self-incapacitated. Something similar to it, however, suffuses my life upon occasion; distils itself in me, one or two tears at a time.

One morning in the course of that parched summer I awoke at about half past five or a little earlier; ready to work, I thought, or almost ready. I was trying to write an essay on William Butler Yeats, based on my notes for a lecture that I had given two or three times, entitled "Story Underlying Poetry." It was a matching-up of the chronology of his life, particularly his strange love-life, with the order in which his love poems were written, obscured by him in the arrangement of his successive volumes but on record here and there, in biographies and critical studies. It interested me exceedingly, but it was work promised and dutiful, therefore my instinct was to put it off.

First, I said to myself, first, let me jot down something about the look on the face of a young or youngish man who had appeared to me in a dream, just on the verge of waking; one whom I knew but had not seen, scarcely thought of, for several years. He had been a friendly acquaintance of my close friend John Connolly, and now and then, when I went to New York, he came around to visit us after dinner. He liked me; liked my being a writer.

For my part, he mystified me which, as I am a virtually professional student of humankind, is often a factor in my sociability, at least for a while. He had an athlete's physique, grown soft. He had a worker's hands, but dressed with some elegance. He was pleasant company, although as a rule he only questioned us and commented mildly on what we told him; volunteering little or no subject matter of his own.

Struck by my making telephone calls to New Jersey upon two or three occasions in his presence, he wondered why and to whom. My way of life with relatives seemed strange to him.

A girl he knew had read his palm and he showed me what she had pointed out to him: right hand and left hand very different; and

I saw and touched the indentation of a wedding ring, deep between calluses. Why wasn't he wearing it?

"How dare you and John find each other?" he wanted to know. He envied us our friendship.

One night he inquired whether authorship didn't embarrass me, when surely all the great beliefs and profound experiences had been dealt with by the classics, the Bible and the Greeks and the Romans and their direct successors. "Life isn't all greatness and profundity," was my answer. Surely the first principle of literature is to behold in nature and human nature little things that the ancients had not encountered or had not noticed or cared about. When he had asked to come and visit us he sometimes made us wait, which John especially resented. Once when he had done so, he calmly explained that, on his way, he found himself half inclined to stand us up; he stopped at a bar and had two drinks while thinking it over. Apparently he regarded us as a temptation, a strong temptation. The next time that happened, John, his Irish eyes glittering, his happy voice suddenly inflamed, upbraided him. He immediately reopened the door through which he had just come and sprang down the stairs into Fifty-ninth Street. I never saw him again, except for the dream that prompted these minutiae of memory.

The dream itself was not in the least dramatic or circumstantial. It consisted, in a doorway of mine, on a threshold of mine, of a motionless standing figure and a silent face. Save for something rapturous in the turn of his neck, the lift of his chin, the tousle of his hair, I could not have identified him. I saw him by his own light. What I saw, or imagined, was a life turning on its own hinges, exalted for the time being, or in remembrance of the time, all about nothing; and as it faded upward in my morning arousal it was not an emotion, it was a moral or a lesson.

As follows: Again and again one is told, and very likely one tells oneself, how fortunate and enjoyable it is to be at peace in one's psychology, single-minded, wholehearted. Then and there between stuporous slumber and hot daybreak, with the above details of personality, inconsequential but congruous, the meaning seemed to be the opposite. There the lost friend or non-friend stood, having blushed to come, refrained from coming, scrupled and delayed, but come anyway. One aspect of himself, after a struggle, had surrendered to another aspect; at least there was a truce. What he had been thinking of as a weakness of character, he suddenly recognized as strength of temperament; and it thrilled him. Two characters could scarcely be less alike than he and I, and yet this was something that in making certain moves in my own life, transitions of fact, or changes of heart, I too had found thrilling.

And, believe it or not, it took me the better part of three hours to ponder this and to note down my findings and musings; useless scribble which I afterward threw away. Perhaps its use has been to lead to the pages that I am now writing and re-writing, twenty years having passed. Verbalization, even unsuccessful or partial, is conducive to memory.

The routine of life with my aged mother in those bygone days was that, having bathed and dressed and put up her beautiful hair, she would ring a little bell, which was amplified and conveyed from her end of the house to my room upstairs by means of electric wiring; whereupon I would go down and breakfast with her. And that morning as I gathered up my neglected, postponed Yeats notebooks, that bell seemed to tinkle with guilt, not just because I was not quite ready to join her—it signified time and energy wasted, caprice and deviation, bad enough in life, worse in literary work.

I paused on the stairway where there was a window at elbow-height, and gazed at the beginning of another day of burning heat and desiccation; the kind of weather that probably would have settled it, if it had not been settled anyway, as to our being dispossessed and inundated, in short order. Already, in Somerset County and

Middlesex County and Union County, I heard someone say, it had become forbidden to water anyone's garden.

Farewell, I said to myself. Farewell, large golden lawn! Here and there, where my housekeeper's brother had cut it too short, a week or a fortnight ago, the sun had burned it to the roots; it looked as dead as a mineral or a metal, golden in that sense. No breeze blew, I observed, except in one small tree in the hedgerow. But it was not an exception, there was no breeze: that was the mulberry tree, with avid birds breakfasting on the white fruit, shaking the small stiff branches.

Closer to the window stood an aged crab-apple tree. Farewell to it also, I thought, noticing that it had one broken bough with dead leaves hanging loose. Perhaps, after breakfast, I would bring the long rickety sectional ladder and the dull saw out of the garage, and remove that bough. There were also several disgusting tents of gypsy caterpillars that wanted burning.

At that moment our male catbird of the last couple of years, whom we recognized and loved because he had two or three notes more than the regulation song of his family, came dartingly around the garage and perched there. I wanted him to eat some of the disgusting caterpillars; he did not. He sang, so ecstatically that when he got to his high notes, he threw his head all the way back and pointed his bill straight up to the stricken blue sky. Upon which I shed tears, and it occurred to me that whereas my sadness had been building up for some time about the drought and the drowning of our valley and uncertainty as to our home (possibly several homes) in the years ahead, what had actually triggered that little moisture in my eyes and on my cheeks was love of the bird, delight in its freakish bit of song, tears of joy, not altogether unlike Pascal's tears!

It was in early September that the brook entirely ceased. I remember standing on the lawn, amid the above-mentioned colorless reflections from the moribund grass, like moonlight intensified, and suddenly I noticed the hush, all around the house, in the entire space amid the trees. For just a second, with a twinge of hypochondrical fear, I fancied myself afflicted with sudden deafness. But it was the opposite of deafness; I was hearing a combination of small sounds that, normally, a general auditory fabric hid from my ears: sighing of the half-dead sod with my feet weighing on it; once in a while, slight thuds of apples falling; and tiptoeing movements of unnoticeable tiny insects.

The missing generality was the brook: its gurgle and foaminess over the stones, its silky rush where there were muddy passages, and the precipitation of its slight waterfall into its dim pool. Having lived near it for twenty years I almost never consciously listened to it. Now, what I was hearing was the vacancy left behind, the bereavement.

I wandered over and looked down into the pool, deeper than I had known it to be: a big mud hole with steep sides of slimy soil and only a foot, or a foot and a half, of opaque water. There lay a great dead eel as long as my arm; and beside it on top of the water, its mate, weakly undulating, not dead.

September, I remembered having read somewhere, is the eel's migratory season, and was not the belly of this still live one somewhat silvery and polished-looking, and were not its pectorals dark and sharp, physical symptoms of its wanderlust? Down to the ocean and away to Bermuda and the obscure weedy Sargasso Sea, from which they never return, but from which they send back their spawn to exactly the fresh water that was home to them in the first place, even my brook! Now, would the living one, if it lived, make the Liebestod voyage without its mate?

My brother came along and found me brooding upon the two eels in the muddy water—the apparent difference between life and death only a slight tone of skin, a soft nervous undulancy—and he knew what to do to save the live one; characteristic of him. The twelve inches of water ought to suffice, he thought, except that probably it was devoid of oxygen; so he pulled the garden hose across the lawn and aerated it.

A little later my housekeeper's brother arrived and offered to dip up the live one in a pail and to take it down to Mulhocaway Creek, which was not stagnant, and he did so. Dear housekeeper wanted to cook and eat the dead one. "I can tell by the smell whether it is nice and healthy or not," she said. I dissuaded her. Suddenly that afternoon it occurred to me that Yeats had felt the importance and enigmatic truth of the small inhabitants of the countryside somewhat as I do. For example, in the summer of 1938—his grandiose old heart aching with expectation of his death—he wrote one of his few poems of pathos, "The Man and the Echo." His identification in it was with a creature even more commonplace than my catbird or my eel, namely, a rabbit. Perhaps, he thought, self-tormentingly, he was to blame for certain tragedies of the past. Was not some of the blood of the Easter Rebellion on his hands, because he had written provocative political poems? Had not his adverse criticism caused the dancer Margot Ruddock, whose poetry was not as good as her dancing, to go mad? Hush! he said to himself in the last stanza; he had lost his theme. Sorrow interrupted it: natural self-pity, because he was dying, taking the form of compassion, of oneness with other victims of life and death. He felt sorry for even the commonest and pettiest.

> "Up there some hawk or
> owl has struck,
> Dropping out of sky or rock.
> A stricken rabbit is crying out,
> And its cry distracts
> my thought."

I think there has never been a lyric poet to match him. In beauty of language, in imagery, in prosody, he is as enthralling as Catullus or Baudelaire, with twice their life-span, and a range and quality of intelligence far more interesting than theirs. Never do I go to the oracle of his lifework in vain, even casually, to verify some quotation or to inform myself about this or that Irish matter. Suddenly a page, a page that presumably I have never before read attentively enough, will cry its wondrous meaning to me, strike home in me with its truth, touching my very soul.

Even a sort of extreme foolishness about some things seems not to detract from his importance and splendor. I like to say of him what he said of Schopenhauer: ". . . he can do no wrong in my eyes—I no more quarrel with him than I do with a mountain cataract. Error is but the abyss into which he precipitates his truths." In many respects, historic respects especially, as to the fate of our immediate family of nations in the West, he has a very pessimistic soul. So have I, and since the time of his death, certain hopes that he still held have deteriorated and new reasons for fear and anger have developed for us, worse and worse.

He said, "We only begin to live when we conceive life as tragedy." One of his foolish perturbations was a lifelong and absolute impatience with Bertrand Russell, the philosopher. "He fills me with fury by his plebian loquacity," he told his closest friend, Olivia Shakespear, and said to someone else, ". . . he has a wicked and vulgar spirit." When it came time to send young Michael Yeats, aged nine or ten, to school, he drafted an imaginary letter of instructions to a schoolmaster, specifying what the small boy was to be taught, and what not. For example, Greek, but no Latin. No history, no geography. As much mathematics as possible, for a comical reason: he himself, perfectly certain that Russell was a featherhead, never had had enough mathematics to prove it, and wanted his son to be able to.

In view of this prejudice, it has pleased and impressed me to find that the extreme Irishman and the noble philosopher-mathematician have had in common a definite tragic sense. Russell told his biographer some years ago that the secret of happiness is to face the fact that life is horrible, horrible! "You must feel it deeply,"

he said—and he beat his breast a little, the biographer reported—
"and then you can start being happy."

When I was in my late teens or early twenties, a rather grandilo-
quent essay of Russell's, entitled "A Free Man's Worship," meant
more to me than any other philosophical writing. Now that I am a
post-mature man, with changed taste but unchangeable mind, in
the deteriorating, alarming, angering circumstances of the world at
large, this anecdote of the breast-beating nobleman means more to
me than that essay meant then.

For needless to say, I am trying—I was trying, all that parched
and bitter summer of 1957—to apply philosophy not only to the
drowning out of a New Jersey valley, and to sorrows of the animal
kingdom, catbird and tent caterpillars and eels and rabbits and the
like, and to sorrows of my own, mostly having to do with limitations
of my talent, weaknesses of morale, but to vast dark historic prospects also. For, needless to say, the remainder of the twentieth century may turn out to be worse than anything that the human species
has experienced to date, with all sorts of effects of untrue religion
and unwise education and irresponsible experimental science, and
democracy perhaps too slow and soft a process to compete with
various more recent bodies politic, with no diplomacy worthy of the
name, and insufficient defensive preparation, flying our strange,
competitive relative kites in the stratosphere like lunatic small boys,
setting up our vast radioactive firecrackers by remote control or
perhaps no control; nuclear physics perhaps a lethal gene, if not for
the entire species, at least for those of us who lead the complex
modern life, in areas of concentrated population, in (so to speak)
the northwestern portion of the world.

Therefore, in the northern and western nations, both in general
and in particular, the spiritual situation is that the soul is in love
with reality, absolutely in love, but throughout eternity can never
forgive it, never, in the nature of the case and in its own human
nature cannot, will not, must not.

Sorrow, truthful sorrow, is not unhealthy for the mature human being. Resentment, vain combativity against fate inside one's own head, is the perilous habit. "When men are very bitter," Yeats said, "death and ruin draw them on as a rabbit is supposed to be by the dancing of the fox."

Poets and other men of the arts, he said, are not "permitted to shoot beyond the tangible," and I somehow believe that this is so— but who or what forbids it? Mere feasibility of form and style, I guess. The poem or the tale on one's desk, the picture on one's easel, coarsens and weakens when one grows too theoretical or argumentative, though in a good cause.

The idea has to come with the image or we seem not to be thinking straight. There is no cause and effect in the abstract. The questions we ask, and the answers we try to give if you ask us, are all a matter of what has happened or is happening. Theory of the future only vexes us, unless it is based on some confession and forgiveness and self-forgiveness of what has gone by.

Thus, all the days of our lives, Yeats said, we have to go from desire to weariness, then desire again, then weariness again; and we "live but for the moment when vision comes to our weariness like terrible lightning . . ." Vision like lightning, messages of the far and absolute reality like thunder, and dread epiphanies of flood and drought and fire and ice, and indeed of mushrooming atomic cloud and other such novelties—or it may be some less dramatic manifestation of the inhuman, non-human, extra-human truth.

It is one of the solemn peculiarities of this century that small persons like myself, great persons like Yeats, get grief-stricken by fears of science, on which war and peace are based, and fears of politics, fraught with cynical hypocrisy and unrealistic optimism. I intend to stop shivering. No one can escape dying. No one has to die more than once.

I have known vision to take the form, the forms plural, of mere low-class or no-class sexual intercourse, not even authorized by

majority practices or justified by true love; mere beauty of dancers'
bodies resulting from nothing but exercise and keeping time to
music; poetry more transparently intelligent than prose, and vice
versa; prose more sonorous than verse; mere paintings that are not
even pictures entitled this and that and the other subdivision of the
palette, and yet arousing in the mind's vain-glorious sunrises or
the opposite, funereal sunsets of the gods—all epiphanic!

Now, 1978, nothing is left of my house in Union Township, except
broken foundations under utilitarian water. I haven't forgotten, and
I expect never to forget the exact way the sunrise appeared in my
bedroom window there, at second hand as it was a north window,
encompassing a certain panorama of the half-wooded, thousand-
foot Musconetcung Hills. In early October of 1957, to my astonishment, my old crab-apple tree re-grew in smaller format some of
the foliage that the caterpillars had devoured, and it curtained my
window quite closely. But the rough showers that relieved our
drought at last, at the end of October, followed by gusts of wind in
the first week of November, drew the curtain back; so that I could
see all that lofty part of the landscape from my bed.

There was an unusual and beautiful place almost at the top
of it, a juncture of wood-lots and upland pastures, which made me
think of someone's forehead, with dark hair growing down in a
widow's peak. Just below that, my neighbor Dalrymple's son and
daughter-in-law and daughter and son-in-law had two small-frame
houses painted white, closely adjacent, appearing to be one and the
same structure. At daybreak, that is, in the quarter before daybreak,
from some point below the horizon in the east or the southeast, the
preliminary sunbeams would arch up across the valley, behind my
back, over my head, over my house, illuminating those houses of
my neighbors first of all. Suddenly I would see them at the foot of
my bed amid the darkness: the sunrise singling them out, before it
had actually risen anywhere else, pouring itself into them, and

transfiguring them into magic-lantern architecture, palaces of porcelain, as in a fairy tale; or as it is described in the last few pages of the Bible, New Jerusalem, battlements of glass and pearl measured with golden reed.

Some mornings the sun seemed to fall back to sleep, once or twice before it actually got its stride and started up the sky. Having delivered its distant greeting and fixed its god-like gaze upon the conjoined Dalrymple dwellings, and the last bit of hillside to the right and left of them, it would stop and let just one or two more drowsy clouds pass, one or two lapsing shadows, with auroral breezes inhaling, exhaling—then it would recover consciousness, take on effulgence and color; stronger every instant but less thrilling every instant, until it had achieved daylight—prose! And as all the rest of the earth and sky, groves and farmland and outcroppings of limestone and rough hedgerows, lit up realistically, the Dalrymple house faded back to mere clapboard and paint and cement block and shingle.

Certain mornings, as I propped myself up on pillows and sipped my first black coffee, endeavoring to wake all of myself up at once, talent and morale as well as *joie de vivre*, self-respect as well as self-consciousness, all that vicarious aspect of the new day—the great response of the landscape to the light while my eyes were still dim with sleep and dream—gave me a measure of that satisfaction which others (they tell me) derive from regular religious observance, prayer or rite or mystical exercise.

In an almost religious mood, in that autumn of 1957, I resolved that for the remainder of my tenure of the doomed house—twenty years of occupancy dwindling down to a matter of months, weeks, days, hours, minutes, seconds—I would like to keep track of the time of the sunrise and set my clock accordingly, so as to allow myself ten minutes of vigil, supplicating, grateful, self-pitying, self-forgiving, in the dark. After that, welcome to the day again, daily, airy divinity of the rays of our particular star, light ever-seeking and ever-finding, symbolizing that certainty which comes most naturally to the imagination, to the effect that happiness exists, is here, is there, is somewhere, which is what matters; giving one occasion to pretend, auto-suggestively, that it does not matter much whether or not one is happy personally.

Naturally, in those vigils, I also resolved some new practices having to do with literature as such: for one thing, to try to curtail what is called inspiration, ideas of things to be written, and to give three quarters of my time and energy to just workmanship, especially the reworking and finishing of a quantity of my scribble of years past. But, I exhorted myself, let there be no ambiguity or uncertainty as to what work or works I have in progress. Let me always have a plan, to be changed if and when my power of execution happens to change or fail, but without making a mystery of it.

While I would reveal myself to my heart's content, I vowed that, for the time being at least, I would stop my self-criticism. Especially I decided to refrain from writing about my writing, or about my failures to write. It is unhealthy for the eye to gaze into itself; a stupidity for the pen or pencil to annotate itself. The difference between subjectivity and objectivity is only form; but it is one of the great differences. Whatever is not (or seems not) narratable can be turned into aphorism or lyricism.

Also it occurred to me to beware of letter-writing, as one of the poorest of the categories of self-expression, almost invariably given over to seductiveness of some kind, and to apology, diplomacy, and didacticism. The letter-writer is always something of a lover and something of a politician. Where there is so much personal purpose there is not apt to be sincerity enough. "The rhetorician," Yeats said, "would deceive his neighbor, the sentimentalist himself, while art is but a vision of reality."

I must admit, realistically, that while indefatigable and immense in my correspondence all my life, I am not, never have been, never have thought myself a very good letter writer. It is one of my miseries, one of my mysteries, underneath the good fortune and the delectable duality of being a city mouse as well as a country mouse and blissful bookishness and retrospective longing and other components of the self-portrait that I have been painting in these pages.

I still write letters. Not to do so was one of many good resolutions that in the elapsed twenty years have availed me nothing. Nevertheless I believe that resolving is worthwhile. It is an education and an exercise. I could if I would describe eloquently, with titles and casts of characters, a couple of novels that I have not produced, with good reasons for not having succeeded at them. As a rule, disappointment in oneself, frustration, renunciation, are a vain wasteful reverie, a slothfulness. Wreckage of manuscript may provide good substance for another piece of work. A vow or a promise will sometimes arouse an unknown, unexpected talented part of the soul. What one does then may be the opposite of what one took oath about or was inspired by, and failed to accomplish and didn't even have the sense to abandon until one had tired oneself out. No matter; in literature as in life, what happens is of greater worth and consequence than the vision and the will-power and the dream.

And now, as this strange-shaped essay draws to its close, petering out, the word "dream" gives me pause. That nameless young man, unhappily hesitant in the dreamed doorway, joyfully entering the room and then, having irritated John Connolly whose room it was, departing in haste and disgrace, what did I mean by him or about him, almost at the start of this reminiscence and self-depiction? Nameless, yes; I now add to my small memory of him that he called himself by two names, and neither of them, as we learned later, was true—but not meaningless.

He was a personification of my Self with a capital S, vacillating at the end of my early middle age, the beginning of my later middle age, with downright elderliness in prospect. My life, leaving out infancy, seems to divide in thirds, not in halves or quarters. To my slowly awakening mind the dream suggested something of the difference between prose and poetry, the one impinging upon the other, with as many of their senses as possible, grasping my being of two minds, my double-meanings, my heart divided against itself. In passages like this, I want others to read as they please, to think as they please, even against me. Furthermore, when a prose piece of any length is composed in a style as specific and compact as mine, it is good to have something in it unexpressed, even ill-expressed, or inexpressible. I like my readers to enter into my thoughts, to sense my emotions, the way mere forgetfulness may bring about some slight elements of fiction in the most honest, earnest literary work.

Landscape is easier than self-analysis. Forty or fifty feet of water lie wavering and flashing and darkening, according to the hour and the wind and the sky, over my brother's and sister-in-law's house; fifteen feet over mine and my mother's. I used to go there often. The last time, I walked along the shore, as close as I could get to my once happy abode, close enough to throw a stone out to it, and in fact I threw one. A young, stout, disrespectful state employee ordered me back to the road. I did as I was told, without any exhibition of grief or irritation. Only I vowed not to go there again. Another lapse of the exact truth; another promise to myself broken. That wasn't the last time; I sometimes take visiting friends there and I point out landmarks around the water and I explain things. But I scarcely look and I turn off most of my memory.

Displacement and resettlement may teach one not to despair too quickly, even of great changes. In almost every respect the good fortune that I have emphasized throughout this essay has persisted. Let me not exaggerate my happiness. My mother did not live to see the actual flooding of our valley. Now, as you may know, my all-important sister-in-law has departed this life. The death of those we love when they are old and ill cannot be regarded as tragedy. It is just loss, like the contents of what was once Mulhocaway Farm and its affiliate reservoir (that natural cup huge and deep).

I remember the day when Spruce Run Reservoir claimed its first victim: a fifty-five-year-old fisherman unable to swim, in a ten-foot aluminum boat which capsized. I recall some of the hapless friends who frequented the valley in our time: Margaret Harrison who looked in her mirror when she was young and, observing how good-looking she was and how cruel looking, like, perhaps, Messalina or Media, determined to behave accordingly, and her little son Norvil who wanted to die and soon did—whereupon she took her own life because she could not bear the thought of what she had done to him. And Michael Miksche, who all one year, 1943 or 1944, bombed Berlin twice a week, a genius-type with very little talent and little education, and George Platt Lynes who greatly loved, and let love go, because it bored him, and died of a broken heart, and Dorothy Hotchkiss, a childlike, childless, and amorous young woman snatched by cancer from the embraces of her young husband, my nephew Bruce, whom in his infancy, in the summer of 1929, I took care of because both his parents were ill. I wondered if their spirits still inhabited that impounded water, strange mermaids and mermen, and perhaps, in envy of the living, with that sad capriciousness which indeed they all had in common, reached up from the drowned fields and overturned the irrelevant fisherman. I never entirely believe any such thing, but all around me I always see metaphors expressive of truth; it is my habit, it is one of my specialties as a writer.

A Call on Colette and Goudeket

Love is a secondary passion to those who love most,
a primary passion to those who love least.

Walter Savage Landor

When I went abroad in 1952 and called on my old and dear friend Cocteau, who was Colette's neighbor in the Palais-Royal, he told me that it had been one of her most dolorous weeks; her arthritis clamping down tight and chiseling away at her. In spite of which, he thought, surely she would receive me, especially if he telephoned and asked her to. For various reasons, I scarcely wanted his powers of persuasion so exercised in my behalf.

Later in the week I found Anita Loos, the dramatizer of *Gigi*, dining at Florial's, out beside the fountain under the honey locusts, and she confirmed the bad news of the arthritis; nevertheless, she encouraged me. "Don't write," was her advice. "M. Goudeket, the guardian husband, will think it is his duty to ward you off. Just take a chance, ring the doorbell. At least you will see him, or you will see Pauline, the perfect servant. They're both worth seeing."

But I could not imagine myself standing all unannounced on their doorstep, nor think of any suitable initial utterance to the doorkeeper. Then I recalled the fact that when my young friend Patrick O'Higgins wanted to get in and take photographs of her, he armed himself with roses. With neither his infectious half-Irish gaiety nor his half-French manners, perhaps I could afford an even more imposing bouquet, to compensate. I sought out the major florist near the Palais-Royal, and asked if they knew which size and shape and shade and redolence of rose Mme. Colette favored. They knew exactly: I forget its name; it had a stout but not inflexible stem, and petals wine-red on the inside, brownish on the outside.

In the doorway the perfect servant gave me a good look and concluded that she had never laid eyes on me before. I held the roses up a little; I thrust them forward. It brought to my mind an encounter once upon a time with a fine police dog when, thank heaven, I had in hand a good thick slice of bread for the purpose of conciliation. I made polite statements about my not really expecting Mme. Colette to see me but, on the other hand, not wanting her to hear from M. Cocteau and Mlle. Loos or anyone of my sojourn in Paris and departure without having paid my respects. Pauline evidently regarded this as all hypocrisy but appreciated the style of it. She took the roses, forbade me to depart without being seen by M. Goudeket, ordered me to sit down and be patient, and went away very neatly.

The Palais-Royal is a quiet building. I could hear a heavy chair being pushed back somewhere; I could hear footsteps along a corridor, certainly not Pauline's footsteps, heavier and not so neat. Facing me was a double door composed of panes of glass backed by permanent light-colored curtains, which made everything there in the hallway rather bright but nothing really visible.

"What is it, Pauline? Who is it, Pauline? But no, but no, not that vase, not for roses. Oh, they're magnificent, aren't they? So long-legged and in such quantity! Leave them here on my bed, for the moment."

Though the farthest thing in the world from a young voice, it had a sound of unabated femininity, and it could never have been livelier at any age. It was slightly hoarse, but with the healthy hoarseness of certain birds'; nothing sore-throated about it.

"Who brought them, Pauline? What young man? The one of the other day, the Swiss one? But, my poor dear Pauline, if he's gray-haired, what makes you think he's young? If only you'd remember names, so much simpler."

Thus she sputtered or, to be more exact, warbled, and I gathered that Pauline withdrew from the room in mid-sentence; the hoarse and sweet phrases murmured to a close. Presently I heard a manly mumble of M. Goudeket, meant for me not to be able to understand; and presently there he was with me in the hallway, welcoming, at least half welcoming.

He declared that he remembered me, which, remarkable man that he is, may have been the case. "As for Colette," he added, in a sort of aside, "I am afraid she is not in good enough health to see you."

Using his arm like a great wand or baton he motioned me into a room which appeared to be *his* room, where there was a display of bibliophily and an important desk.

In France I always observe a great difference between politesse and just politeness. Politesse is stronger and can be made quite uncomfortable for one or both of the participants. M. Goudeket seated himself at the desk, assigned me a chair vis-à-vis, and questioned me for half or three quarters of an hour until he became convinced that I truly, unselfishly, loved Colette's work and would continually do my best to further a general love of it in vast and remunerative America.

I told him what I thought: a number of the most interesting titles for export to this country had not yet been translated (still have not)—especially her reminiscences, which ought to be combined in one fat volume, suitable for a large-circulation book club. I went on to say, in a less businesslike manner, that I could not think of any autobiography by a woman to compare with this work of hers. Most women, throughout literary history, have been rather secretive, therefore objective. Not even Mme. de Sévigné is in Colette's class for width and depth of revelation, for fond instructiveness, and for poetical quality. This comparison, though perhaps hackneyed, seemed to gratify M. Goudeket.

Then I mentioned Colette's particular gift of brief wise commentary, epigram, and aphorism. As a rule this is not one of the abilities of the fair sex. Logan Pearsall Smith's famous *Treasury of English Aphorisms* included, if I remember rightly, only two authoresses. This information made M. Goudeket smile.

As soon as cordiality prevailed between us, our conversation flagged. Despairing by that time of seeing the beloved authoress, I looked at my watch and alluded to the fact that I had another engagement, beginning to be pressing.

This apparently astonished M. Goudeket. "But I thought you wished to pay your respects to Colette," he protested. "Surely you can spare just a few more minutes! Speaking for Colette, alas, I am afraid she will be deeply disappointed if you don't."

He said this with rare aplomb, disregarding what he had said upon my arrival, exactly as though, at some point in our interview, he had been able to slip out of the room and reconsult her about me, or as though she had communicated to him by telepathy.

"Colette has changed her mind about seeing you," he said. "She is feeling in rather better health today than usual. Come, we will knock on her door." He knocked good and hard and then ushered me in. He addressed her as "dear friend" and he called me "M. Ouess-cotte."

Let me not flatter myself that the great writer had been primping for me all that half or three quarters of an hour; but certainly I have never seen a woman of any age so impeccable and immaculate and (so to speak) gleaming. Let me not try to describe her: her paleness of enamel and her gemlike eyes and her topknot of spun glass, and so forth. There was evidence of pain in her face but not the least suggestion of illness. What came uppermost in my mind at the sight of her was just rejoicing. Oh, oh, I said to myself, she is not going to die for a long while! Or, if she does, it will have to be sudden death somehow, burning death, freezing death, or thunderbolt of some kind. The status quo certainly is life, from head to foot.

She arched her neck back away from me and turned her head somewhat circularly, though in only a segment of circle. She worked her eyes, staring for a split second, then narrowing them, then staring again, so that all their degrees of brightness showed. She gave me her hand, strong with lifelong penmanship as well as gardening and the care of pets.

"Please sit on my bed," she said. "Yes, there at the foot, where I can look straight at you. Arthritic as I am, it wearies me—or perhaps I should say it bores me—to turn my head too often."

Oh, the French euphemism, which is stoicism in a way! Evidently it was not a matter of weariness or boredom but of excruciation. A moment later, in my enjoyment and excitement of being there, I made a clumsy move sideways, so that the weight of my elbow rested on the little mound of her feet under the coverlet. She winced but did not scowl. I apologized miserably, which she put a stop to by pulling the coverlet up above her ankles, in a dear humorous exhibition.

"Do you see? I have excellent feet. Do you remember? I have always worn sandals, indifferent to severe criticism, braving inclement weather; and now I have my reward for it, do you not agree?"

Yes, I did remember, I did agree. She exercised the strong and silken arches for me and twinkled the straight, red-lacquered toes.

On the whole, I must admit, our dialogue or trialogue was not very remarkable. I had been warned of her deafness; indeed the beautiful first page of *Le Fanal Bleu* is a warning. Now, as I try to recall things that she said, I find that they were not very well focused on the cues that her husband and I gave her; she only half heard us. She devoted all possible cleverness to mitigating and disguising the vacuum between us, and therefore did not shine in other ways, as she might have done in solo performance.

Naturally her husband knew best how to pitch his voice for her ear, or perhaps she could somewhat read his lips. "M. Ouess-cotte thinks your autobiographies will have the greatest success in America," he said.

"Oh, has he read them? Oh, the Americans are greater readers than the poor French, aren't they, monsieur?"

"M. Ouess-cotte is perhaps exceptional," her husband murmured sagaciously.

"Have you read *Le Pur et l'Impur?*" she asked. "I happened to read it myself the other day and I took pride in it. I believe it to be my best book. It is the book in which I make my personal contribution to the general repository of knowledge of the various forms of sensuality, do you remember?"

I remembered so well that I recognized this last sentence as a quotation from it, almost word for word: *"Le trésor de la connaissance des sens . . ."* It is a work of gospel truth to my way of thinking, and has greatly guided me in my own life and love life.

When we fell silent M. Goudeket gave us a helping hand, a helping sentence. "M. Ouess-cotte suggests that I ought to make a selection of your thoughts in aphoristic form which I should find here and there throughout your work; something like the *Pensées* of Pascal or of Joubert."

"But no, certainly not, my poor friend! You know perfectly well, I am no thinker, I have no *pensées*. I feel almost a timidity and almost a horror of all that. As a matter of fact, thanks be to God, perhaps the most praiseworthy thing about me is that I have known how to write like a woman, without anything moralistic or theoretical, without promulgating."

And she expressed this bit of negative feminism in an emphatic manner, with her sweet voice hardened, sharpened. "I am a genuinely womanly writer," she insisted. "I am the person in the world the least apt to moralize or philosophize."

I felt challenged by this seeming humility. I, as you might say, took the floor and discoursed with eloquence for two or three or perhaps five minutes. I can recall everything I said, but, for some strange reason, I seem to hear it in English, not in French. Is it possible that in my opinionatedness I slipped into my native tongue without noticing? I seem to see Mme. Colette's face turning masklike, as though she had suddenly grown much deafer; and M. Goudeket, than whom nobody could be less stupid, looked a little stupefied.

It amounted to my giving her the lie direct. Whether she liked it or not, I declared, she was a thinker, she did philosophize. In volume after volume she has enabled us to trace exactly the stages of her development of mind, her reasoning in its several categories and connections. The gist of it may perhaps be called pantheistic; a cult of nature which is no mere matter of softly yielding to it, which infers a nay as well as a yea, and which includes, yes, indeed, with outstretched arms, all or almost all human nature. Of the utmost importance to her is, quite simply, belief in love; the particular passion in due course giving way to general loving-kindness, amor giving way to caritas, amour leading to amor fati. A part of it is just spectatorship and dramatic sense, with no admiration of evil, indeed not; only an appreciation of the part of that evil may play in fate, as among other things it occasions virtue, and a willingness to yield to it in the end, when worse comes to worst, when it takes the form of death.

Suddenly hearing myself talking so grandiosely, and mixing my languages, my few words of Italian along with my French and/or

American, of course I stopped; and then it was time to bid the great woman and her good husband au revoir. They very kindly urged me to return to Paris before long, and she undertook to rise from her bed when that time came and to lunch with me at the restaurant just down the street, the Véfour, where she had a corner table marked with her name on a brass plate.

I departed with a lump in my throat, with a very natural dread of old mortality. But then I reminded myself of the printed form of immortality, a sure thing in Colette's case. I stopped at a bookstore and bought *Le Pur et l'Impur*, though I have two copies of it in New Jersey, one very cheap, for rough-and-ready reading, and one well bound, for the sentiment and the symbol. I immediately cut the pages of this third copy, not wanting anyone to observe it uncut in my hand to shame me by supposition that I had not yet read it. I walked through the Tuileries and up along the Seine hugging it (so to speak) to my heart.

Sacre de Printemps

A story inspired by J. Hatfield and his friend Mason at Oxford.
Written I think, on my trip with the Goldmans.
Berlin probably, after seeing J.H. in Oxford.
Influence of Mary Butts.

G.W.

The body of one was monumental and colorless, Goethe's dream of Apollo; the body of the other was immature, rust-yellow and sharp. On fibrous cane a terra-cotta blossom bloomed. But the wood they squatted on was wet.

The afternoon, ending, turned colder. To remark this, to compare their comfort, to conclude, to rise and go in one direction, being intimates, required only a movement, an ascending spark in their eyes. One transferred his weight to pillar-like limbs and, not even pulling his hands from his pockets, stood erect; the leap of the slenderer, pushing his palms on the emptiness around, ended in a slight lurch. They turned toward Oxford.

Editor's note: An experimental, surrealist story, written in 1923 at age 22.

To the memory of learning: eternally solid stone boxes, holding books, hearths, beds, benches, all priestish, chambers and stairways whose staleness had long been a perfume. No fountains or distorted Virgins, but an infinite variety of doors; Inigo Jones in the exquisite style of a skull; and infinite combinations of lovely brutal Gothic and Roman in its three sober variations. Essence in a pan of bonelike rock, sour draught drawing through the corridors and laborious climbs; reflected on bald eroded wall an inbred intellect begotten too many generations by the same book. Hemmed in by this stone-work, the full gardens without an erotic trace, none of the symbolic boy; *(the gardens of Adonis were so empty that they afforded prover-bial expression, and the principal part thereof was empty spaces, with herbs and flowers in pots)*; but thick vegetables made to celebrate preceptor and unripe intellect in visible hymns, squat leaf developing upon leaf, and prostrate flowers full of hidden stamens. A few chapels, in the old rock-like knife-cut dew, spoiled by Cromwell. What was ugly, as the pocky geraniums and the cat mutilated by drunken sons and, between college and college, the brick shops and homes where the vulgar sweated and bred and wept, presumably against their will, were held by mutual consent to be meaningful.

"When you say atmosphere you mean detail," remarked Hamilton, the muscular one, somberly, as if it were law. Valentine's strange face glowed.

Being Americans they were haunted by America, *the beautiful*: federated valleys of stinking rivers overhung by rickety steeps; cement obelisks with fine steel bones; Blue Laws and Negro boys being burned; wealth, and premature ripeness of exhausted males, of females like porcelain and "two-faced." "God mutilate America," MacNeill had prayed when drunk. "Remember the Aztecs, remember the Negroes and Pueblos and pacifists. God give their women to the blacks, keep increasing cancer, burn their theaters full of yet green children." A bloody fight was due. To determine the quality of something not yet wholly differentiated from what has gone before: Amen.

The contrary was their life: to be despised, to be ignored, to be bullied by an air. To submit to tyrannies, policed indoors at ten, and discomforts, as wet beds and gritty baths, and poisonous diet of cabbage and cold-storage meat. By comment consent; a blessing, to those who had done nothing with masses of men but shout. The gaze here had to be frozen, as prepared for tormented god and, when expectation died, preserved to ward off impertinence. Not a soul, not a friend was to be greeted in the open air. Slapped on the back in Nebraska, they were grateful; belonged, between burlesque and maudlin feeling, to a company whose foreheads were countless as pearls of gravel, but whose love could be made exterior only by the pitch of their voices, faultless, pseudo-Doric chord.

The ancient Puritan, first bred here, was propitiated by the spare joy. The wounded eye, blessed by Henry James, unable to endure its yard and ditch, made of this, statuary; art not life, so the distortion caused no pain. Mouths without appetite or satiety, eternally closed; Greekish faces meeting one another without impact as geometrical lines meet; reticence, as a mannerism of a school of actors, false and lovely; a cold-bitten waste, smelling of hounds, created around the upholders of stale decencies. The pitiful Americans possessed no causes.

Reddish and pinched as if by cold, some affected chapped skin and never to be newly shaved; shabby wool, in which rain beads and does not sink. Hamilton had not abandoned his middle-western styles: too tight suits which creased horizontally from the buttons, and flannel-padded ties, sharp shoes and a vest-pocket full of pencils, pens and patent nail-files; but Valentine enjoyed a black flannel shirt and electric-blue string of silk. Unconsciously an imitator, of eccentrics the gravel and damp lumpy beds also bore. These had Javanese cotton printed with jungle-hens and ovals pointed at one end, and handles of their silverware were of a pre-Gothic animal with the hindquarters of a worm. Men also haughty, some miserably exhausted, but abstracted as if hearing something measured and shrill. One had egg-shaped violet eyes and a mouth like a dead poppy. These were the objects of wit they hoped was normal. Hamilton and Valentine discussed the old evil and new conscience; took the correct position, from the Germans.

The curd-white path unrolled. Pines in spring, the soft one hung with mustard, another a black steeple; and a squat hawk-colored bush. The always shaken-up lilacs started with seedy dark buds. Magdalen's tower, heavy with shields and rosettes, put up. Along water they wandered, slime-heavy, scratched by twigs and rotten strips, drab dank flood.

Behold, the swan. Not a bird, not a bird. Pallid and bleak, sudden, breaking everything, floating, turning. Recollections of snow rose, foliage of glacier, old stiffened honey—they fell down, serene, heavy, in Valentine's head. He was appalled, by what he named the bird's beauty.

A barge of feathers, scale on scale, white which is fusion-of-colors, water-proof, dragging a shadow of black, absence-of-colors; sea-going breast, uncleft breast, all the plumage and the immense elbows covered with down and hung from these bones the oiled linen and woodwork of a giant kite, all the plumage wrought toward the back, where it rose steeply, many-leaved, out of the water; within, black greasy meat, washed in unclean blood, a few bladders of food and slime to be ground by flints; but coiled muscularly on the atmosphere above, the limb of its centuries of power, the neck, the snowy rubber-hose with nib of horn black as ebony.

Breathing heavily the air parted and made shiver the feathers. Silent, plunged its long throat through the soft flood, and perhaps mouthed the umber muck. Deep under the perfumed little-limpid fluid its Negro-black feet beat the waves stored invisible there, and these paddles spread their vibration through every quill and small whittled bone. Linked to filth, stainless; and hung in the dirty shadows, heatless light. The bird caught in its strangely placed buttons for eyes the adoration of man, and exhibited its beauty; swayed its shoulders, revolved rigidly, gave itself deeper into the water, put out its neck straight and hard like a tulip.

"Beautiful," Hamilton said, in a small tone. Then Valentine escaped; from the holy animal that had been a lizard.

They hurried, on the lawn of Winchester, through its fruitless stone. Drained, tricked, subdued; the captivity had been terribly good. And after, a peculiar world, in noticeable perspective like a stereopticon view. What his eye saw was exaggerated so that the intellect also saw. Striding with the motion of one wading through the common life of animals, vegetables, architecture, and men, his friend. Unmixed, of the nature of an element one could call by a capital letter. A man haughtily built: blunt muscles attached without subterfuge to regular bones, interlocking types of flesh and skin of several tints, excellent and harmonious. He watched him walk, and, less eagerly, watched himself walk, as if it were a difficult, a curious performance. At the same time, distracted, he felt that he would break in pieces but for Hamilton, a bulwark to resist sensation. The inside of his head already reeked with fever.

They clattered in the gutter at twilight between houses baptized with bloody color of brick, and recoiled from the acid moisture of their hall, and pushed inward their door, the literal, the carpenter's idea of door.

Martha Sloe sat there, hands clenched, weeping. Red and sodden against sunken green wall. Getting up, a mere blot in Valentine's eyes, she appeared to trample the exhausted hearth; and facing Hamilton commanded him pitifully, "Come with me."

Valentine jumped for his hat and stick. "No, you stay, I'll go. I need a book, the Union closes . . ." She took his hands, shaking the tears from her head. "Dear Arthur, dear Arthur, you are good. But your room has murdered me already. If I didn't deserve it . . ."

They were gone. Arthur turned very cold and rushed around the room. Fed the fire, filled his pipe, lit it, emptied it. Poured whiskey in a cup, spilled it in the geraniums. Squatted on his feet, painfully cold; cold like marble. Busied himself with the girl, facts he knew: Canadian, dancer in nightclubs before 1914, husband killed in the first month of the war, child dead of something hideous, married again, to a young Communist, and mother again. "I loved my deformed war-child so that I can hardly care for the common lovely one," she had said. He was sickly suspicious of his pity. The fire licked him, doubled his cold.

In the sitting-room of importance. American son of pallor, exhausting bigotry and shame, he knew well his father: Methodist minister, whiskered priest, warning blandly against Socialists and painters. One morning he had fainted in the road, with pulpy ears full of sand; the seven-year-old boy thought him dead, and sat on the sod, relieved and inhuman, watching the horse-flies buzz over the swollen face. Impotence: to regard other men as muscular and fertile, to buy their tolerance with wit, to wait; to dry up, to go stale, never to know hunger. He was picking at the beauty of boneless fingers, he was a kind of sea-anemone. To build up a slim passion by reflection on the nudes of art, and to watch it wilt. All the wildness and sharpness concentrated in a minor affair, like that beastly bird; then left without a souvenir, and with no idea where to look for it again. The parlor repeated his sickness, in scrollwork, plush tassels in colored marble like sausage. Thank God for Oxford, for decency, for tradition which matters more than private fate, gaiety or belly-aching, for reticence and death.

Hamilton returned. He asked no questions, out of cowardice, but smoked desperately over Matthew Arnold. MacNeill arrived.

"Pall-bearers who have not been introduced. Apparently you think it good form. Mope only before a Hindu or Egyptian, he will regard it as moodiness of god. This is a school for empire. You may as well get the maxims right." He had an elegant, calamitous face, with broad lips covered with fine wrinkles.

"At any rate, Oxford has a mind, a collection of faiths which dominate," Hamilton insisted, stretching his weighty torso.

"My dear Leonard, can you tell why we are here? Taught to rule, nothing to rule. Taught to behave like a royal family, to awe inferiors, with the inferiors all dead. Carriage of lions, brains of capons."

"And I may dine at journey's end with Landor and with Donne," droned Valentine.

"Indeed you mayn't. Not if you rot here with the remains of English Worthies, and go home to teach. To be a little spout of the false Water of Life, mixed by philanthropists, a stinking patent medicine. 'Whoever shall drink of my blood . . .'" He glared at poor Valentine.

Hamilton interrupted. "What is Herbert Sloe writing?"

"A forecast of our century; translated into seven languages, including the ideal war. Women's innards bursting out of their own accord. Miles of standing men, stinking, like the husks of dead crickets. Villagers choking to death, or ripping one another open with pitchforks and axes in a stampede over a puddle to slake their hydrophobic thirst. Sloe hopes to horrify the workers into knocking Lord Curzon and his friends the profiteers on the head, I suppose."

"And what are we to do?" Valentine cried venomously. "Not being keen to knock . . ."

"Prepare to meet your God, fool; prepare to die. In other words, amuse yourself." He was very shrill, and the smile on his curious face frightful and exquisite. "In fact, the increase of degeneracy may save us. Since we haven't an outside enemy to fear . . . Europe is one body, the mouth gnawing the legs, the hand ripping the gullet, eating its freshest children. What doomed the Greeks is our hope. Degeneracy: I mean rotting of the aggressive forces, the infirmities of grace and tolerance, courage, rare in strong men, pity and luxury. The gluttonous old men, Foreign Office and munitions workers can exploit all the heroic animal virtues. Only divine weaklings can spoil their game."

"The icy bowels of the interested . . ." recited Valentine from Beckford. "The rigorous hand of the man of business." Hamilton looked annoyed and felt weak and hot.

"Given a pitiful temper, your course is plain. Undermine, undermine. Honeycomb the sword with taste and skepticism, and scorn all corruption, till it collapses in the hand of whomever it profits to use it. Rot the competitive strength of men. Sabotage their reservoirs, make their ideals so elegant that they cannot bear weight, spoil, spoil. Then the hordes of Russians . . . And we shall be here to tame them. A few parasites in the barbarous tents, but with the body of our faith . . ."

Beyond this, his mouth could not improvise. In the darkness the bells began like heavy pulses. They went out together.

Night stippled and stained, muse of chemists in sweaty towers. "Here lies the dead love, the dahlia toe," in rococo script on waxy slabs, on the tombstones in Boston. He saw over a lumpish stream full of heads and chopped-off feet, livers and tongues, a huge fisher standing like a clothes-pin. Hallelujah. Despicable intellect, he said to himself, not even the founder of your own anguish.

Out of the pitchy sky came exquisite gray breakable columns, clasped to the raw street at its edge. A lamp flared and quailed under an arch. He wanted Michelangelo's woe of muscles, he wanted sobs breaking out like an avalanche; not his corpse of an intellect chewed and worried by dogs. MacNeill was the curse of God. They found a pub.

The walls were plastered with engravings of hunters and dogs as an envelope with stamps. In a hideous hearth a pair of coals, the conventional corrective of an outer sky swelling and sagging like the bag of a balloon. The whiskey had an odious flavor, but the burn excited him. Three men: one hiding a mere fact from the others, one trying sickly to tell his own mind something, one baring the repulsive body of a reality bitterly loved, who kept on pitiously. "You are a painter. And why don't you paint?" MacNeill went on.

"It is true that I studied two years at the Art Institute in Chicago," Valentine groaned.

"And then?"

He leaned against the thick wreath on the mantel like a design in dough. Valentine imagined his friend's hands weighed down with deep-bodied roses, blackish and dense roses, wondering at the inappropriate notion.

"And then? And then?" MacNeill cried as if he were a tuneless trumpet.

"I tired of the hallelujah atmosphere: contention, scandal, appetite. I am a modest organism, do not enjoy such hot palpitating air. Raw, nothing old, nothing inevitable, nothing renounced. Paint what—ugly land the color of an artichoke and flabby women. It is an impropriety to mix thought and experience; in the west there is no institution to prevent it. And all my friends, when unoccupied, battered at my decencies and habits, tireless primitives. At last I couldn't draw a firm line, and stopped."

"There is another sort of art," MacNeill said dreamily. "There is Paris; and the hundred heads in all kinds of stone of Mlle. Pogany— thought that is identical with experience, or experience that is thought. Matter or experience, revolting, perfidious, or just insufficient, the lovely and atrocious insanely mingled—it is there, lies there, like the drowned body of someone you have loved; and you can stoop down and put your mouth to the loose wet one, and breathe into it, breathe life into it.

"Not I, far from it . . . The product of irreproachable ideals: asceticism and nationalism, the Jesuits and Mrs. McBride. You may have heard, I am a Sinn Feiner. A boy I loved was shot in the stomach in Wicklow, is said to have dragged himself a quarter of a mile, leaving a track. How could I paint? You know what Ireland is now, split again by the women and that holy New York Jew DeValera. Even the Home Office knows I am done for, and lets me go where I like. But—if I were an American . . ."

The stones without set up a moderate uproar under someone's feet. Valentine wrung his hands mechanically.

"So you are leaving Oxford?" Hamilton asked with guarded perspicuity.

"Of course," he laughed sourly. "To Paris. To sit in a room like a bullpen, a room with an immense chandelier with claws precisely over my head, my aching hollow head, adding columns and licking stamps. For thirty-five francs a day, till night. To eat bread that is not gummy, to breathe scented air, to be a little drunk, to make love, flatly, comparatively, as a man compiling facts. A minor spoiled Joyce."

"I have read it, I have endured, I have held on, like a cowboy with his teeth in a bull's nose," Hamilton boasted, trying again to arrest the intolerable monologue.

"Marion Alpha and Omega, Marion the Blessed Damozel?" the Irishman murmured, as the woman was paid, and, feeling like a troop of men, they marched into the black street. In the darkness, a jagged leafage divided by roofs and light, they heard in that acute voice, the voice of a saint in pain, a theory of *Ulysses*: Stephen the first theme, treble and terrible, throat of a fallen angel, blackened with old beauty, old theory; Bloom the second theme, loathsome and kind, "the man in the street"; the first, tragic by excessive aware-ness of the other's evil, the second, tragic by unconsciousness of his own; developed and intricately combined, as a sonata, in the fantasy of lusts and the chapter like the catechism; closed by the chorale of

Marion, who was before and will be after, leveling the heartbreaking contrast. "The revenge of two phases of man upon each other," MacNeill muttered, beating the payment with his stick.

Neither could listen to him any longer; but Hamilton, having detected his friend's misery, rested one hand on his shoulder, exactly and insubstantially, as if in bewilderment of his own misery, over-looked or unknown to others.

The thought rose and began to stir violently in Valentine's mind: this was the hand of a prince "and whoever shall threaten the free-dom or mar the peace or cripple the habits of such a one, inheritor of all kinds of pride and primitive grace and uncompromised power, is despicable and corrupt." Therefore his sleep was heavy and impure, holding him down; the thought changed to "whoever shall do or say something horrible heard in the chattering, almost speech, of an animal, which in unutterable agony could not be understood, shall be whipped by an enraged priest or father, with a drop of spittle in each corner of his mouth." So he would hold his tongue.

The friends met at breakfast, Arthur's face like a plaster cast of itself. "Great heavens, boy, you do look as if you'd taken vows." Leonard grinned gently as they sat down to the leather-colored tea, the rolls they called "bricks without straw." "That Irishman of ours . . . He's fanatical, fanatically intelligent. And the worst of it is, there's a pitiful look about him, which says he can't help it, and begs you not to avoid him."

"I say the worst is, that he's not a fool," Arthur complained. They went bicycling.

No traces of the stained spring, the mouldy and pitiful mass in which the swan had appeared. Roads of damp silver-grey gravel rose and fell on hills which drew themselves up with a lovely small no-bility. The sky painted with watery blue; and between small plump clouds, yellow sunlight was let down as if in a net. Many larks, after their effortless elevation, hung above, apart but in tune, and seemed, by the sound, to bloom and shake out pollen.

England, England . . . "Lovely word," Arthur murmured. Oceanic island; who can forget how it lies in the sea, lies deep in the sea, like an overfreighted boat, fragilely, eternally moored? In the sea and of the sea and almost under the sea: trees like giant swaying shrubs, boneless and dim; blossoms beneath, all circular, with toothed edges, candid and small, nearly of shell; never startled and never angular cattle, drifting over a dreamily-moulded meadow; hills echoing the waves in soil. Even men move with a peculiar smoothness as if, like fish, their lives depend not on effort but on harmony, an inherited harmony with what surrounds them.

The light wet and strong, a substance mobile and severe; and as they moved swiftly on their bicycles, the bodiless horses of taut wire, it seemed to part the distance and make it shift, branch on branch, as a current pushing through submarine plants.

Arthur was stirred by the meaning of the landscape, but the movement was too headlong and laborious. His course became more and more like a tunnel, polished walls of glassy air streaming by and the floor plunging toward and under him so that he thought of falling on his face, a tunnel with a trembling speck which was Hamilton constantly snatched out of his sight by turns and valleys. He began to peddle with his mind as well as his legs.

The road suddenly vertical on a hill with some feathery trees. Leonard stopped and waited; they walked to the top. But Arthur's mind, inflamed by fatigue, had no rest. Through it, frantically, the aspects of the man beside him rushed, not to be held, acute and inexplicably acute. The few glittering hairs on his wrists; the neck a cylinder rising at right angles from the collar bones, a pair of hard leaves; the head at once conventional and disturbing, with weighty eyes and schooled hair; the burned pallor and deep red. To each image was attached a value or quality; loyalty, courage, patience, to the hands compassion. The total had been friendship, now a chaotic sickness; his friend lost in a heightening and division of sensibility.

The little winds prowled around the top of the rigid hill, toothed and dripping. There the road went down, a pallid rut in the underbrush. Off again; again buzzing in his ears, and the hopping hotly desired speck in his eyes. Unequivocally down.

A small animal, perhaps a rabbit, crossed the road in front of him. He couldn't bear it: swerved, struck a rock, struck a tree; his weight got very far away, not over his feet; his position suddenly blew up, exploded.

Beyond this accident, he did not join actual experience immediately, without a seam; the day was cut open and a panel set in. In it he crouched down over a spring shaped like a pear, and tried to hold the cold prickly water with his hands, which made him very unhappy. While this went on he did not open his eyes, but they were open, and only big enough to hold Leonard's face, near and apprehensive.